TUNNEL

BRIAN DYKO

ISBN-13: 978-1490334608
ISBN-10: 1490334602

Manufactured in the United States of America

–To Leslie, my love; and to my mother–

Table of Contents

Part I: The Tunnel – p.7

Part II: The Chaos – p.29

Part III: Los Angeles – p.63

Part IV: The Island – p.133

Part V: Cleveland – p.197

PART I: THE TUNNEL

I

Alex plunged the needle into his index finger. Letting his wound bleed freely onto the plaid couch, he passed the needle to Stella. She stuck it into the tip of her finger, and let the needle fall to the floor.

They touched their tips together and shared their blood as they kissed and swore eternal union.

The power of their blood oath shot through the roof of their third-story apartment, into the nighttime sky. It soared past the earth's atmosphere and into outer space. It glided by the sun and its planets, and headed for the black hole at the center of our galaxy. Within the singularity of every black hole lays the border between time and timelessness. And within that border rests the realm of the Chaos.

II

Neither Alex nor Stella had ever made such a magnanimous gesture before, and were left looking at each other and wondering what was next as their blood ran through each other's bodies. His deep blue eyes absorbed the ecstasy and awe in her beautiful brown eyes, and reflected it back at her. They stayed in this trance for countless moments until Stella at last suggested.

"Let's paint something."

They got the acrylics out and placed a medium-sized canvas on the ground.

"So what do you want to paint?" he asked her.

"Paradise," she replied with a smile and a shrug, and made a broad violet brushstroke of an arch.

"Now you go," she said.

Alex accentuated her arch with a soft yellow one that fit snugly under hers. He silently invited her to make a move. She offered a shiny blue blob that hinted at a pond, and Alex more clearly defined it with green specks that suggested themselves as shrubbery.

As they neared completion on their pastoral scene, it started to rain quite heavily. And then the lighting came, and soon the thunder followed.

Alex grew kind of melancholy.

"What's wrong?" she asked him.

He shook his head sullenly, "Nothing."

She looked at him, half-pleading and half-concerned. There was no point in resisting her.

"It rained just like this eight years ago today…the night my mother passed away."

"Oh Alex," she embraced him, "I'm sorry, I never knew the day."

"I guess it's still hard for me to talk about."

She nodded in acknowledgment.

"I know it is."

"I just wish you two could have met, that's all. You would have loved each other."

There was a moment of silence.

"I know it might sound crazy, but I feel as if I do know her, through you. And I love her very much. Sometimes I could swear that I feel her presence here with us, but I don't want to say anything about it because I don't want to upset you."

He did not offer a response right away, but kissed her on her forehead and held her body closely to his own body.

III

Elizabeth was in eternity, a part of a whole with no individual thoughts or desires. A fullness so full it was closer to nothingness. A place that was not a place. Conscious, yes, but contained within the context of the whole. She wanted nothing. Expected nothing. Existed as billions before her now exist – ethereal, amorphous, timeless.

And then when the blood oath her son had made with Stella cut through the Chaos and reached into the sphere of eternity, she was awoken. It was the only oath ever powerful enough to penetrate the barrier of timelessness and coat it with its essence. Reinvigorated by the sensation of coming back into contact with her own blood, Elizabeth's spirit separated and floated away from the whole. She did not know why her spirit was independent again, but by instinct traced the tear the oath had made back to the point where the sphere of timelessness began.

There was a hole in the border, but only large enough for Elizabeth to see through with one eye. Through the hole she saw utter darkness and confusion. And something down there seemed to be breathing, but erratically.

"Hello?" She called out, "Is everything okay down there?"

Leaning in closer to try and hear it better, she lost her footing and fell through the hole into the realm of the Chaos.

She dropped through the darkness for some time before she hit solid ground. When she picked herself back up, she noticed that she could no longer float freely around. In fact, she could only walk now. She could see the hole from where she had fallen, but realized that there was no way for her to get back up there.

From the hole in eternity, the path the blood oath had torn into the Chaos stretched way off into the opposite direction above her. Not having anything else to guide her, she followed underneath it.

IV

Alex sat at his black desk with crumpled papers scattered all around him. He had been there for hours now. It was quite late, and Stella was peacefully sleeping in the other room.

Stella was in her last semester of college, while he had graduated a few months ago. He had the rare good luck upon graduation of being offered a book deal with a national publisher. Over the course of undergrad he had completed a manuscript, submitted it, and gotten an offer. There was a condition, though. Parts of the main plot and a few of the characters needed to be re-worked to more easily fit into the current market demographic the publisher had in mind for Alex's story. Try as he might, though, he couldn't seem to make these simple changes. He had already turned in a few revised drafts, and each time the publisher told him close, but no cigar. In fact, they were growing impatient with him now, and told him in no indefinite terms that if in three weeks he did not have what they were looking for, they were going to pass on his project.

So he couldn't blow it. Not only would it destroy his confidence irreparably, he and Stella were poor as hell. Her student loan money was already practically gone, and they had no other source of income. This book offer was his only opportunity. If he messed that up, he'd probably find some job somewhere, eventually. Hopefully. But he'd be a shell of who he once was.

Stella did not put the same kind of pressure on Alex as he put on himself. She loved him unconditionally. And

14

because Alex knew this, he didn't want her to have to love a loser.

Feeling stir crazy trying to find inspiration in the only room of their apartment other than the one Stella was sleeping in, Alex decided to take a walk. He went into the bedroom and gently kissed the top of her long amber hair. She seemed to smile as he re-tucked the sheets around her.

They lived in the thick of the campus housing that rested just north of the university in Columbus, OH. It was a short walk to campus, and Alex figured that maybe the beauty of its landscape and architecture might be enough to inspire him. He walked around the university for a while, but could not clear the void that blocked his mind. Eventually the fresh air made him tired, and he headed back home.

He laid his long body to rest next to Stella, who unconsciously purred as he joined her under the covers.

V

Elizabeth stared at the gash in the Chaos as she walked below it. The strange breathing noises she had heard before she fell from eternity seemed to be coming from there.

She was distracted by it, and did not notice that a giant funnel cloud was rushing towards her from the side. It overtook her, and tried to shove her back through the hole in the border between the Chaos and eternity.

The hole was rapidly closing in on itself, though, and she was not fitting through. The energy increased around her and made a greater push, but still could not do it. Then the hole closed completely, and she dropped back to the ground. She lay there, crumpled at the feet of a tall shadow man.

"Immortal trespasser!"

He bellowed down at her. She looked up and saw that the shadowy figure wore a crown, and that he was holding a small tornado in his hand.

"I demand you state your business, or be ground out of existence!"

VI

Alex was back on the university quad, standing on the neatly trimmed grass with no shoes on. The art building was on fire. A blue blaze surrounded it, but did not seem to be consuming it.

Screams were coming from the basement. They sounded like children. Alex ran towards the building. The screams were getting louder as he neared a tunnel that led under the main entrance. He ran down the eastern staircase, into the fire. It was not burning him, though – it wasn't even hot. But the screams intensified.

A cartoon man was graffiti'd onto the wall of the tunnel. He had two heads, in profile, looking away from one another. One orange and one red. They were the one's that were screaming. They had spiral eyes and their mouths were howling in pain. The heads shared one neck that spun down into one red orange body.

Alex scratched at the wall to try and peel him off, but he seemed to be trapped inside of it.

"How do I help you?" Alex shouted at him over his screeching. "Please, I don't understand how to get you off this wall."

And with that, the man lifted his red right arm off of the wall, and pointed across the tunnel to a room that led into the basement of the art building. A locked steel door closed it off from the tunnel, but there were two windows that looked into the room. As he peered through them, he knew at once that the source of the fire was in this room. It was so bright in there that it was like looking into the sun. Alex tried again to open the door, but it was definitely welded shut. He turned back to the man, who was still pointing at the room, howling in pain.

"It's shut, man. What do I do?"

The man's arm grew longer, as if to emphasize the door leading into the room. Alex tried to grab the extended arm to yank him from the wall, but his arm was nothing more than a hologram. He went to pull the door once again and it felt like it was finally giving way. But then, as often happens in dreams, Alex was somewhere else entirely.

He was on the banks of the Cuyahoga River. It was the river that ran behind his childhood home, a few miles back into the valley, and eventually spilled out into Lake Erie. He was standing at the bend in the river where his mother's ashes were spread eight years ago. His family was there, as they had been during the actual funeral ceremony, and he watched as the water at the bend flowed in every direction at once while his father prayed before the scattering. And then he woke up.

The sun shining through the blinds was what woke him. The morning light had roused Stella, as well, but she was far from fully awake. He reached his arm over her shoulder and spooned her from behind. He stayed awake with his eyes closed, breathing the scent coming off the back of her neck where it met her auburn hair. And they lay there together for some time, facing the sun as it came down on them through the window.

VII

Alex and Stella ate a breakfast of eggs, toast, and coffee. Afterwards, they made love and took a walk around the block. It was a beautiful summer day – hot, humid, and fragrant with freshly cut grass and the singing of birds. Her long hair cast a purple tone as it bounced around her shoulders, and her eyes sparkled as she talked and laughed.

When Stella stopped so that she could more intently gaze upon a branch of low-hanging yellow tree flowers, Alex said,

"You know, I just can't tell."

"You can't tell what?" she asked.

"Whether you're stopping to admire the flowers, or if they're stopping to admire you."

She blushed.

"You're really on a role lately, aren't you?"

"I got a way with words. You should tell that to the publisher."

"I'll do more than that. I'll send them a bomb in the mail if they mess around with your story much more."

They both laughed. "Thanks, Stella."

Then she looked at him like she was looking at the flowers a second ago – with wonder and tenderness.

"All kidding aside, though, how are you doing?"

"Just fine. What do you mean?"

"The other night was the first time that you really started opening up to me about your mother, and then you just kind of dropped it. I don't want to push the issue or make you uncomfortable, but I don't know, I guess I

19

want to make sure that you're doing okay and that you know you could always talk about her with me."

"I know that and I really do appreciate it, but let's just enjoy the walk for now."

He started walking away from the tree, but she did not.

"Sometimes I wish you had some faith in something," she called out to him.

He turned around. "I have faith in you."

"Then let me lead you to her," she implored him.

"How?"

"Do you realize that in the year or so that we've been together, you haven't shared a single fond memory that you have of her? Only how sick she was and how sad it made you. I know you have something happy in there, and I think it's important to share those things before you lose them."

He looked off into the distance and tried channeling something inside himself.

"There is this one time that I always come back to, and at this point, I'm not even sure if it really happened or if it was in some dream that I had. But I have this memory of sitting on a swing with my mom on this old black deck that we used to have. Everything seemed just right. It was warm and sunny, and this giant willow that we had in our back yard shaded us. I don't remember what we talked about or how old I was at the time, but I remember the smell of the air. It was crisp, alive. Almost like the ocean was filled with raspberries, and somehow able to reach us in the suburbs of Cleveland. And we gently swung as the sound of waves rolled in with the breeze."

He stayed in that place for a few moments before coming back to Stella.

"That was lovely. Thanks for sharing it with me."

He was choked up, but managed to silently acknowledge her gratitude.

"It's okay to be sad, Alex."

He wiped away a few tears.

"I know it is. But when I think about the positive things, it almost makes her death, and death in general, seem more real to me."

"Are you afraid of dying?"

"Of course. A little. But it's more—" he looked her in the eyes and couldn't bear to say it.

"You're afraid that I'm going to die?"

He shook his head.

"I'm just as scared to lose you," she said. "But we can't dwell on what might happen. We are here now, together, and I love you."

"And I love you too. But honestly, I don't know what I would do if anything ever happened to you."

She grabbed his hand and squeezed it tightly.

"That's a good start for now. Let's walk by the lake and try to see the baby ducks before I head to class."

***

When he got back to the apartment alone, he set his mind to start revising his manuscript. He sat down at his computer desk, and without thinking too hard about it, gave it a go. It was not long before every stroke of the keyboard frustrated him, though. Not yet losing his cool, he brought out a notebook and tried working the old-fashioned way. Ink on paper. Surely he could draw inspiration from that. It was such a romantic method. But alas he found himself, pen in hand, staring at a blank notebook. He was no closer to any sort of progress.

He flipped open his phone and gazed upon a picture of Stella by the Scioto River at sunset in the fall. He loved that picture of her. If he could not find inspiration in the love of his life, what business did he have being a writer anyways? But her image just made him feel happy and lonely. His story was that of a nineteenth-century Western mystery, and he needed to channel feelings of wonder and awe. And danger and suspense and confusion. Not puppy-dog lovesickness.

And then the glowing room from his dreams suddenly burned into his mind's eye. And he could hear the screaming once again. It was getting louder and louder in his head. Was that graffiti man inside the tunnel wall actually real? Was he still suffering? Was the room really there? These were questions he did not know the answer to, questions that elicited the same kind of mood he was trying to convey in his novel. He picked up his notebook and headed to campus.

***

Sure enough, as he walked down the steps below the main entrance to the art building, it led him into the tunnel from his dreams. The red and orange graffiti man was there, and so was the door leading into the basement room. It was indeed welded shut, but there was no light coming from inside of it, so the narrow windows alongside the door only showed darkness.

He walked back up the staircase and then entered the building's main entrance. He took the first flight of stairs that he found down to the basement level. There were a few lectures being given in small classrooms on the north side of the basement. The doors were open and he could hear the one professor talking about cubism and its relation to the war. There was only one room on the south side of the basement, and its door was closed. That was the room he wanted to get inside of. In that room existed the inspiration that he needed to write. He was sure of it.

Alex tried turning the doorknob, but it was locked. Of course. He looked around for a needle or a hangar, something to pick the lock with. There was a pen on a table in the hallway next to the room. He twisted the bottom of the pen off and removed the ink tube from inside it. He tried jamming it into the lock and moving it around to trip the latch.

"Excuse me?"

A man's voice called out to him. Alex turned around and figured the guy to be the professor from the class across the hall.

"Um, yeah?" Alex asked, trying to play it cool, attempting to hide his pick.

"Can I help you with something? Or should I call campus security?"

"No, uh, that's not necessary sir. Sorry about that," he looked down and saw that his hands were covered in the black ink from the tube he just busted. He walked away without looking back at the professor, who stood there in the middle of the hallway with his corduroy jacket on until Alex went back up to the main level. His phone rang. It was Stella.

"Hey babe, where are you?" she asked him.

"Oh, you're back already?"

"Yeah, we got let out early today."

"Okay. I'm on campus, but I'll head back. I'll see you in a few."

"Alright. Love you."

"Love you too."

And then Alex washed the ink off of his hands and returned back to their apartment.

VIII

Amongst their circle of friends, Alex and Stella were renowned for their cupcake making abilities. It was Tanya's birthday, a sort of bland, but nice girl in Stella's film studies program, and she had requested red velvet cupcakes for her party. Alex and Stella were more than happy to oblige. Baking was very calming to them both.

They had already set the butter and eggs out for about a half hour so that they would get to room temperature. They then sifted flour, sugar, baking soda, and cocoa powder together into a green bowl. Stella whipped the butter in a separate bowl, and then Alex added the eggs. Slowly, the milk, the extract, and the sifted ingredients were added to the butter. The red dye was added to the batter and then scooped into greased cupcake trays before being placed in the oven.

"What film do you want to watch?" she asked him.

"Hitchcock would be cool. Maybe *Frenzy* or *Marnie* – one of his later movies."

"I'd watch *Frenzy*."

Alex took a seat on the couch, and Stella turned the projector on. They did not have a screen or anything, so they just cast it upon their white wall.

She had found the projector, broken, for real cheap at a garage sale. She was good at fixing things, so she bought it, and within no time had it up and running. Which was good, because they watched a lot of movies together.

So they relaxed and watched the thriller. Despite the strangulations and generally psychotic tone of the movie, Alex couldn't help but interrupting it and saying to Stella,

"I really do want to thank you, Stella, for helping me to deal with emotions that I've bottled up for years. Your love is the best thing that has ever happened to me."

"I feel the same way about your love, Alex."

They proceeded to watch the rest of the movie, stopping only to take the cupcakes out of the oven. There was another storm that night, and when they went to sleep, they cuddled very closely together.

***

Since the spreading of Elizabeth's remains into the Cuyahoga River, her ashes had evaporated, fell back down with the rain, and evaporated again many times over. The winds have carried her all over the world, and tonight there was a single ash from her body hanging in the clouds over Columbus.

As it continued to rain, the ash fell down in a drop that landed in a puddle that had formed in the university commons. As the puddle outgrew the dip in the concrete that was holding it, a tiny stream ran off from it and flowed downhill toward the nearest drain. That drain was located at the center of the tunnel under the art building.

When the stream reached the metal drain, it dropped through it and down into the university sewer system below. The grating of the drain was slightly elevated, though, and Elizabeth's ash got caught in it as the water passed by.

***

The sun came up the next morning and quickly dried the puddle that fed the stream. The ash remained caught at the top of the drain. Later that morning, a mosquito who had recently been born down in the sewer below, came up to the tunnel and mistook the ash for food. The fly gobbled it up, but it provided the insect with no sustenance.

Shortly thereafter, Alex came down into the tunnel. He had just tried reaching the basement room through the inside of the building, but once again found it to be locked. On the off chance that the steel door that provided exterior access to the room was open, he went into the tunnel.

He found the steel door still welded shut, but the lights were on inside the room this time around. Through the two windows he could see that the room was painted bright green. The room seemed to be empty other than that. As he was looking in, he didn't notice that a mosquito had landed on his right forearm. Having not been satisfied by the earlier meal of Elizabeth's ash, the insect stuck its jagged jaw through Alex's skin and drew out his blood.

As the blood mixed with the ash inside the mosquito's stomach, it marked the first time that Elizabeth's earthen body came into contact with its living blood since her death. Suddenly the spiral orange left eye of the graffiti man in the tunnel started glowing. It curled off of the wall and reached for the mosquito on Alex's arm. The force of it grabbed a hold of Alex, too, and the next thing he knew was that he was floating through the graffiti man's eye. He was painlessly lifted through the wall, through the ground, and up towards the blue sky above. As he was approaching the clouds, he first noticed the mosquito sucking on his arm and swatted it away.

PART II: THE CHAOS

IX

"I assure you, your majesty, I fell through a hole in eternity and that is all know."

He studied her intently.

"Is this some sort of trick, Lucifer? Distract me while your minions once again march towards the earth at the other side of my kingdom?"

She laughed.

"*Lucifer*? My name is Eli—"

And before Elizabeth could finish her thought, a glowing blue energy suddenly burst out of her and flooded into the gash that cut through the Chaos above them. As it flowed from her, an equal and opposite energy soared towards her from the sphere of time. It lifted her up through the darkness, and pulled her towards itself.

The King of the Chaos stepped back, not daring to come into direct contact with the currents of energy. Such an encounter would surely end in his destruction. Then again, he would just as certainly be eliminated if this immortal somehow made it into the sphere of time.

The warning God had given him millennia ago was still fresh in his mind. After the fallen angel, Satan, traveled to the earth unchecked through Chaos' realm, the Almighty made it clear that if any entity of time or of timelessness should ever again cross through the Chaos and reach into the opposite sphere, the temporal and the eternal would fuse together and cancel the Chaos out of existence.

So the King hurled a cage of fire at Elizabeth, and trapped her inside of it before she could be drawn any further through his kingdom. The effort sapped his power, though, and caused the gash in his kingdom to widen a little.

"Indeed you are not Satan, for he would not so easily be trapped. Tell me then, weakling, what is this energy flowing through you?"

She said nothing; in fact she could not say anything as the energy flowed through her.

"Tell me, or be reintroduced to pain!"

She could not say a word. Even if she could, she didn't understand what was happening, either.

"Very well."

He closed the fiery cage in on her. She writhed out in agony. It was strange to her that she felt pain, after so long of feeling nothing. And though it hurt, the fire did nothing to stop the mysterious energy from flowing in and out of her.

X

Alex noticed that though he was rising through the clouds rapidly, his ears were not popping, nor did they feel like they needed to pop. It was cold and humid up there, but Alex did not get wet or feel the temperature. The change in the pressure had no effect on him either, nor for that matter, did he feel any wind moving against his skin.

"This is nuts," he said to himself.

He opened his mouth to try and eat a piece of the clouds, but somehow none landed in his mouth. They just went right through him like a ghost.

When he made it to the other side of the clouds and into the clear blue of the stratosphere, he could see cloud mountains projecting up towards him from out of the Arctic sea of cumulus below – like tall waves frozen in motion. Between the mountains, the great white fleece spread out almost limitlessly in cottony valleys that conformed to the earth's circular atmosphere.

Through an opening in the clouds, he saw the unmistakable patchwork landscape of central Ohio – a flat quilt of grass, trees and dirt farms – sewn together with long stretches of highway. He could make out the shapes of suburbs and cul-de-sacs, swimming pools, and areas of industry before the clouds shifted with the wind and obstructed his view once again.

Continuing his ascent, Alex easily recognized the International Space Station when he saw it floating there in front of him. At that very moment, a Russian astronaut aboard the station was performing a space-walk to fix a malfunctioning valve that was making it hard for them to store their waste matter without it stinking up the small, confined space. Alex and the astronaut both saw each other at the same time, and despite the impossibility of human survival in outer space without a pressurized suit filled with oxygen, the astronaut was not even a little surprised at the sight of Alex. He just waved at him, and Alex waved back as if they were old cosmic friends reunited after years gone by.

Behind the space station, the edges of the thermosphere lit up with the green luminosity of the Aurora Borealis. He pointed at them like a little kid would point at something he didn't completely understand but was captivated by. The astronaut followed Alex's directions and turned to see the green wonders. By the time the astronaut turned back around to give Alex the thumbs up of appreciation, Alex had already moved out of his view.

He was quickly closing the black gap between the moon and the earth, coming now within full view of the moon. The sun was behind the Earth, so it was only partially reflecting off of the moon's surface. The toenail sliver that was hit by the sunlight sparkled like thousands of crushed diamonds lying on a showroom floor.

As he moved even closer, the moon looked like a toy marble with its glass membrane removed from it. There was no atmosphere whatsoever, so Alex could clearly delineate the lighter highlands with the darker, craterous lowlands.

In addition to the larger craters, were millions of little bubbles and pockmarks scattered across the lunar surface.

It gave the impression of soda pop being poured and instantly frozen as soon as it hit the glass.

He was showing no signs of slowing down as he came within feet of the rock's surface. He could see that the American flag that had been planted there in 1969 was tattered now, and that the plaque beside it was covered in moondust. As a matter of fact, in only a few moments his head would smack right into that very plaque and he would never see Stella again.

He tried to swim in another direction to avoid the collision, but it was no use. Some invisible force from afar was pulling him towards it. He was truly terrified, and he realized then that he should have just left that tunnel and its stupid room alone. What good was curiosity anyways? It certainly didn't do any favors for that cat.

XI

Stella walked through the door of their third floor apartment, announcing,

"I picked up some new paintbrushes on my way home," and from her book bag placed them on the couch. She looked over at his desk, where she thought he would be, but he was not there.

"Alex? Where are you?" she called out for him.

She checked the bedroom, and he wasn't in there. Nor was he in the kitchen, or the half-closet that he would hide in from time to time to tease her.

"You better not be trying to scare me. I warn you, I'll scream so loud that the neighbors will hear me."

She did a cursory glance of the apartment once more and then pulled her phone out of her yellow purse. She was instantly transferred to his voicemail.

"Where are you, Alex? I thought you said you'd be home when I got back from class. I'll get dinner started. Hope potatoes and tofu will be alright. Love you."

When she hung up, her stomach felt like it had fallen out from her, but she didn't understand why. She sat down on the couch and took a moment to catch her breath. Then she went to the cupboard and pulled out a frying pan, poured some olive oil into it and turned the stovetop onto medium heat.

XII

Alex closed his eyes and curled up into a ball, bracing for certain impact. Well after it seemed like the moon's crust should have flattened him, he opened his eyes to find that he was floating through the spongy catacombs of purple crystal that comprised the moon's mantle.

He passed like a phantom through lavender caves laced with iris and mauve, whose violet stalagmites seamlessly weaved into amethyst stalactites. Each crystal contained explosions of mulberry, cerise, and of plum; sparkles of periwinkle, orchid and phlox.

A gentle source of light shone through the translucent purple rocks. It seemed a little like sunlight to Alex, but how could that be inside of the moon?

Gradually the purple rocks were giving way to duller, grayer tones that were now reflecting the oncoming light more than allowing it to pass through. The light did not hurt Alex's eyes, though he could tell it was getting more intense.

He came upon a giant glowing orb of orange magma at the center of the moon. It reminded Alex of a fortune teller's ball that had just been activated. This must be the core. He figured that he would pass right through it, much like he had done with the mantle, but instead his course steered him around it and into the dark side of the moon.

The mantle of the dark side looked exactly like the mantle of the light side. It was practically a mirror image, with it starting out duller around the core, and then turning into radiant purple prism sponginess as he moved outwards from it. The only difference was a clear blue liquid that was embedded into one of the crystals that Alex was approaching. It looked a lot like water to him.

He passed through the liquid, and much to his surprise, was soaking wet when he emerged from it. As a result, he started getting very cold as he moved further through the dark side.

It was not long before icicles had formed off of his eyelashes. His hands were dark blue and his fingers were practically gangrenous. He tried moving his neck but it was stuck in place. Before he knew it, his whole body had frozen solid. He was not dead exactly, but had become nothing more than a rigid block of ice.

When he broke through the crust and entered back into outer space, his frozen eyes were treated to a transit of Venus across the sun. Though darkened by the Sun behind it, Alex could make out the magnificent complexity of the Venutian atmosphere – all sorts of colorful clouds and gases swirling around each other in a visual symphony. It was quite lovely to look at, and love is what it made him feel. He saw Stella's face cast upon the surface of Venus. She was smiling at him, and he could practically smell her hair. How he missed smelling her hair. He went to cry out,

"I'm sorry!"

But his lips would not move. He felt the tears trying to form in his eyes, but the ice surrounding him would not allow them to run. Like windshield wiper fluid that froze under the hood in the dead of winter, no matter how many times he tried to pull the lever inside, nothing came out of the frozen ducts.

Venus rapidly moved away from the sun, and left only the great star for Alex to stare at. The strength of the sun's rays melted the ice off of him instantly. In the next moment, they burned his eyes out of his skull, blinding him.

XIII

The King of the Chaos materialized at a safe distance away from the time hole, and watched furiously as the energy flowed through it in both directions. He knew that he could not kill the immortal that had already crossed over, but once the mortal element passed through, he could easily break the current by taking the mortal's life.

But then he felt a slight pull coming from the hole. He backed away from it – yet found that he could not back away quickly enough. The King had never not been in full control of his own body. In fact, he had always been able to freely manipulate every molecule of the Chaos, which within the center of each contained an endless battle between the four elements. But he was losing power now, and getting dragged towards his doom.

He willed himself to teleport to a different part of his realm, an act that normally required no effort at all, but found he was not able. In a desperate maneuver, he manipulated the dark particles around him into an earthen pillar that he clutched to for support, but the hole kept dragging him in, pillar and all.

He morphed the pillar into a thick tree trunk and gave it roots; built land around it to hold it steady, but still felt the pull. To compensate, he gave the land more trees, put a river at its center and raised great mountains up into the darkness. He put suns of many colors into the sky above, and thickened the ground below. Soon the strength of a whole world held him there, but only just barely.

His feverish construction weakened him further, and he found himself needing to rest.

***

As the gap above Elizabeth widened, the fire that consumed her burned a little less hot. Through the still substantial amount of pain, the prolonged exposure to the energy she was receiving put her current situation into context for her. She knew now that her son was approaching – that he was the energy she was feeling. She was not sure how this was possible, but she knew it. His approach was somehow weakening the King.

XIV

Though blind, through the darkness the sun remained visible to Alex in different spectrums of light. It reminded him of when he was a little kid and would stare up at the sun with his eyes closed, but as if he were doing that through high-powered binoculars. He unfortunately couldn't make out any of the sun's finer details, but he could see solar flares geysering out from the sun's surface like appendages stretching out for a second, before curling back into the body.

And as Alex soared closer and closer, he felt like he was sitting inside of an oven. Red walls cubing him in, crushing him, limiting his oxygen. Chest stagnate with stale stuffy air. Thirsty to the point that his tongue had dried up and shriveled into his right cheek. The heat crawled up through his nostrils and boiled the moisture out of his sinuses. The sun kept burning through what little protection the force carrying Alex through space-time afforded him, and soon burned the skin fresh off his bones. His blood instantly evaporated with his muscles, and his bones disintegrated into the vacuum of space. He was now little more than a vapor cloud under the indifferent power of the great star's gravity.

His gaseous self didn't so much as pierce through the sun's membrane, as much as he boiled into it. Though vaporized, he was still very much in pain. It felt like he was underwater, but without visibility, without mobility, entrapped in plasma solidified, pressurized so that each atom of his existence was subjected to the diamond treatment.

The eleven dimensions of space-time were all viewable at this point inside the sun – though Alex was far beyond any comprehension gained through sensory perception. Every dimension was stretched out here, not curled into strings. And the dimensions chopped Alex up into eleven dimensions of his self.

That was shortly lived, though, as the heat of the core exponentially tore apart his eleven different existences piece by piece, rendering him nothing more than a multitude of neutrinos, mesons, quarks and anti-particles.

As he was fused into its nuclear core, the sun's history was mysteriously made known to him. It was born as a third generation star, inside of a stellar nursery located light years upon light years away. Incubated by the supernovas of red giants from the generation of stars before it, spewing their iron and lithium and cadmium insides into the womb that nurtured our sun in its zygote stage. After fusing with the precious, heavy metals, it was born into the darkness of space alongside a twin brother known as Nemesis.

All stars survive in binary systems, with some having more siblings, but no star in the universe is born an only child. And Alex saw how Nemesis and our sun slowly grew apart from each other over time, yet always revolved around one another. The orbits of these brothers lasted hundreds of millions of years before they pulled to their closest point of interaction – which was still lights years away from one another. And how the force of their meeting up with one another was responsible for extinction level events.

Next, he saw the early formations of the solar system we all live in. He watched a time lapse of the planets all form around our sun out of the space dust that surrounded it. And he saw the rise of civilization on the earth, and the fall of civilization many years into the future.

And then Alex was made to know that the sun was in the middle of its life cycle. Once it reached its end, it would become a red giant in it its own right and swallow up the earth and the other planets, but not grow grand enough to supernova. Our sun's fate was that of a white dwarf, a cosmic grave of infinite density packed into an area the size of Manhattan.

***

Slowly Alex felt himself coming back together again within the core. Molecule by molecule, forming around a definite central, solitary existence. First, his cells started taking shape one by one. Then his tissues, like his bones and muscles and skin. His heart started beating and pumping blood throughout his body. And then his eyes opened back up.

When he was fully reformed, the sun ejected him at super speed back into outer space. He looked back at the sun, as it quickly grew distant behind him – this time without any harm to his eyes or body whatsoever. He was reborn in the sun's core, now invincible against the effects of raw space-time.

He quickly passed by crater-faced Mercury and then the red planet Mars. He shot through the asteroid belt and right past majestic Jupiter with its Great Red Eye. Space centaurs galloped past him, as Alex zoomed past Saturn with her lovely rings and giant moon. Next were Uranus and Neptune, and then poor disregarded Pluto encased in ice. Then by Sedna and Eris and the frozen wonders of the Kuiper Belt, straight through the Scattered Disk. Past Tyche and the Oort Cloud, clear out of the only solar system Alex had ever known as home.

XV

Back on earth, the potatoes had just started to golden brown in the frying pan.

Stella was not used to not knowing where Alex was. She had texted him quite a few times, but there was no response on that front either.

She tried calling him again, but only got his voicemail.

"I'm starting to get a little worried, babe. Call me back as soon as you get this. Love you."

She flipped the potatoes with a spatula, and then added the extra firm tofu that she had set to the side. After a few moments, she added some diced tomatoes into the mix. A tear rolled down her cheek, and mixed into the meal. Something was definitely wrong. Should she contact Alex's dad, or his brother, or maybe some of their friends? He hadn't been gone that long, and she didn't want to needlessly cause a panic.

She had one leftover tomato, which she placed back in the pantry next to the cupcakes they had made the day before. And she just stared at the cupcakes.

Next thing she knew, smoke had filled the air, and the alarm was going off. Coughing heavily, she cracked open a window. She covered her mouth with the blue blouse she was wearing and turned the stove-top off. She used a towel to beat the remainder of the smoke out of the window. Then she went to the cupboard and pulled out two plates. She divided the charred potatoes and tofu onto the plates, and set them down on the kitchen table.

She sat down behind one of the plates, and then pulled her phone back out. She dialed his number and once again got his voicemail.

"Dinner's ready. Hope you're on your way."

And then she hung up the phone and sat there before the burned meal, waiting.

XVI

After Alex had been ejected from the sun and out of its solar system entirely, his vision seemed to be enhanced. Strange alien stars and their planets appeared to him in a crystalline clarity. Quasars, pulsars, and supernovas were as common to his view as the Big Dipper and Orion's Belt were to stargazers confined to Earth. Blood red and aquamarine cloud galaxies spread across the pitch black tableau effortlessly. Spiral galaxies in the style of the Milky Way dotted the black backdrop like an array of exotic jewels in a endless cosmic crown.

Yet he found no planet that he passed resembled Earth, even in the slightest. No sign of the existence of intelligent life, either. He had half-expected a flying saucer to pass by him at any moment, but to no avail. Suddenly all of this celestial beauty that surrounded him seemed cold, distant, unwelcoming. Too inhuman. As if he had reached a point in space-time that no human was ever supposed to reach.

With that realization, the clarity seemed to dim. It lessened by degrees until he found himself surrounded by a series of strange swampy flashes, like lightning up close. Like a Jackson Pollock painting made from light yanked out of every spectrum. And for a moment he was stuck in place, as if treading water, and realized that he was staring into the eye of a black hole.

The light was being pulled into the cosmic charybdis, and he could swear that he heard individual photons screaming, and dying, as they passed into the event horizon. He too, was getting yanked at both ends, and it stretched him out like he was made of taffy. Soon he was no thicker than a thousandth of a thread, and like a piece of spaghetti that falls through the strainer and into the drain, slithered into the abyss.

There in the event horizon, the trapped photons behaved like a firework waterfall continuously spawning baby waterfalls off of itself at all angles in a prism. Held there until the end of time. Growing and growing and growing until this black hole swallowed other black holes, and in turn got swallowed by a bigger black hole that would eventually be swallowed by the final black hole. The final black hole would absorb the whole universe and all parallel universes, until it caved in on itself at its infinitely dense singularity, and created another Big Bang to start it all over again, or maybe instead, rendered everything into a state of permanent stasis.

Once he passed through the event horizon, and squeezed through the singularity at the center of the black hole, Alex suddenly found himself traveling on a small canoe upon a river. His body was in its natural form once again, as if it had never been stretched out.

He did not have to row the boat. A gentle current carried him though what can best be described as a psychedelic play land of a river valley. The grass on the river's banks was purple and gold. The trees and flowers were of all different shapes and sizes – pinwheels that reached to the clouds, honeycombs as thin as a needle and as thick as a skyscraper, triangles that revolved and split in half and turned into diamonds. Multicolored mountains, some covered in snow, and some ablaze with fire, gracefully dotted the landscape.

Six suns hung in the sky, all seemingly composed of a kodachrome kind of light. The purple sun hung highest in the sky. The red sun seemed to shine the brightest, but it hung at the lowest position. The pearl, pink, and grey suns all sat in a line that rested just above the mountains. And the green sun was way off to the side, and cast the subtlest shade of light. Beneath these suns were so many wonders, that Alex's eyes did not know where to look.

**

Meanwhile, the King of the Chaos felt the tugging that was bringing him towards the time hole ease up. He let go of the tree he was clutching, and found that he could once again float freely about his own kingdom. He watched as the time hole closed completely. He could sense that this was all a result of the mortal element having finally arrived into his realm.

And on the other side of the Chaos, the energy that was flowing to and from Elizabeth had abruptly come to a halt. She gasped in terror. Being immortal, she knew that the King could not kill her, but she understood that the same could not be said for her mortal son. She hoped that when the energy dried up, his life had not dried up with it.

XVII

As Alex continued to sail along the stream, the land was constantly changing around him. The grass went from purple and gold, to orange and black. The multicolored mountains that were in the distance, now spiraled up below him. Whole trees disappeared, and new ones sprung up in random places. He also noticed that there were no animals populating this land. Not in the sky above him, not on the ground of the banks surrounding him, nor in the water below.

Then without warning, the red sun burnt out like an old light bulb. The sky was still bright, just not quite as colorfully luminous as it was before. Then the green sun went out. And then the grey. And then the purple and the pink suns. Pretty soon the only sun that was still shining was the pearl sun. Somehow the solitary sun made Alex feel more comfortable, more at home, and closer to Stella. But then it too went out. And there he was, floating in the darkness, surrounded by darkness, headed for the darkness.

And though he could no longer see anything, he certainly felt it when a great tidal wave crashed down upon his canoe, and shattered it to pieces. His lungs called out for air, as the waves kept hammering down upon him and slamming him into the river's banks. But then he realized that his lungs asking for air was purely out of instinct. He didn't actually need any air. He was fine. And he didn't feel any pain from being beat against the stony banks, either.

The monarch was infuriated by this. Had he not enough power to kill this puny mortal? He manipulated the dark matter molecules around Alex into a cyclone of fire, and swirled him up like a vacuum cleaner. But it was not burning Alex's skin. The fire should have burned through his bones and vaporized him.

Raging, the King formed the darkness surrounding Alex into the palm of a giant, earthen hand. It grabbed a hold of Alex and closed its grip into a fist to crush him, but his rigid body only chipped away at the rock as it clamped down. Though the stony hand could not squish the life out of Alex, it effectively trapped him inside of its closed fist. For now, the King saw it fit to leave him trapped there. Since Alex could not find a way out of his current predicament, he just sat there and focused on not getting claustrophobic.

***

The King was weakened from trying to kill Alex, and as the gash in his realm widened, the bars that were holding Elizabeth shriveled up. They were in such a frail condition that they no longer posed an obstacle to her escape. She let herself out, and soon realized that she could once again float. Hopefully she was not too late. Maybe she could still save her son from the King.

XVIII

Elizabeth flew towards the sphere of time with great haste. Not particularly to her surprise, the King of the Chaos materialized a few hundred feet before her. He shot off a fresh cage of fire in her direction to re-trap her, but much to his surprise, she countered his attack with a bright blue celestial force that she shot out through her fingertips. She was coming back into sync with her eternal essence, and drew added strength from knowing that she was now fighting to protect her son.

Their two forces fought against each other in a pretty evenly matched battle. It was something of a stalemate, with neither side relenting, nor losing any ground. Then the thought occurred to the King that keeping the mortal imprisoned from afar was diverting his reserve of energy for the present battle. An immortal at full strength is quite powerful indeed, and he simply could not risk Elizabeth getting to the point that he could no longer handle her.

***

The stone hand that held Alex loosened its grip and let him go. He crawled out and walked into the darkness.

The ancients knew what modern science has since complicated, that a unique combination of the four elements inside of all of us is responsible for our own individual thoughts and temperaments. Through these elements, we are all inextricably connected to the Chaos, though few of us know it. Humans have no control over the arrangement inside of them — only a limited capacity to react to it.

Indeed the King, who lords over the dark matter and the elements, has complete control over the arrangement of the elements in any given human. He rarely, if ever has a direct hand in the arrangement, preferring by his very nature to let randomness take hold. But in this particular instance, since he was not able to kill Alex, Chaos set out to manipulate the elements inside of him instead.

In sorting through his elemental makeup, Chaos could see every aspect of Alex's life. He had already guessed it, but did not know for certain until that very moment that Elizabeth was Alex's mother. Though he might not be able to kill Alex, the King now knew very well where his weakness resided.

As Alex journeyed through the nothingness surrounding him, he heard a soft little cry coming from the near distance. He walked towards it.

There, in the middle of the darkness, sat Stella at their kitchen table. She had cooked his favorite meal, though from the looks of it, she had accidentally burnt it. There were two plates prepared, though she sat there alone.

"Stella!" he called out to her and ran towards her. She did not seem to hear him. "I've missed you so much." He said to her and threw his arms around her in an embrace. But they went through her, as if she were a ghost.

"No, please. Please don't do this to me."

He knelt down before her image.

"I don't know if you can hear me, babe, but I'm so sorry. I should never have gone looking for inspiration in that stupid room. You're my inspiration. You're all I've ever needed—"

But as he was talking, her image and the table before her disappeared, and he was left talking into the darkness.

"Don't go. Please don't go. I love you—"
He collapsed to the ground, powerless.

***

Alex had been walking through the darkness for who knows how long. All he could think of was his lost love. This whole journey he had felt pangs of guilt and loneliness and self-loathing, but now those feelings were so intense that they revolved like a buzz saw inside his soul. He only walked, because if he stayed still, the pain would get worse.

And then a loud noise like knives being sharpened against each other inside of a tornado snapped Alex out of his miserable stroll. He looked up and saw what looked like Jupiter's Great Red Eye, floating there before him against the darkness. There was someone inside the anticyclone, but they were so engulfed by it, that they were obscured by it.

Feeling both suicidal from his vision of Stella and indestructible after his last bout with the King, Alex walked right into the powerful storm without hesitation. As he made his way towards the center of the malevolence, he realized in amazement that he was looking at his own mother.

She seemed to see him there, but could not talk. She looked like she was in a great deal of pain. Alex grabbed a hold of her and carried her outside of the prison she had been trapped in. He set her down and just stared at her in disbelief, not sure what to say.

"Hello, Alex," she said to him, and despite all that he had seen up to this point, he fainted.

XIX

It had been a long time since Elizabeth had possessed arms, but that did not prevent her from knowing what to do with them. She went over to her son, who lie prostrate on the floor, and cradled him closely to her as if he were still an infant. She hummed to him and brushed his hair gently back with her hands. All the emotions of an earthen motherhood were flooding over her once again. Protective of her baby boy, she looked all around for the King. Where was he? Alex started getting restless in her arms as he started to regain consciousness.

"There, there my son. There, there," she said as he opened his eyes. When his mother came into focus, he still could not believe it. He blinked rapidly to try to fix what was obviously an error in his brain activity. But still she was there, humming and smiling at him. He rubbed his eyes a few times for good measure, but she was still there. He stared at her in bemusement.

"Could it really be you, Mom?"

"Yes, it is, Alex. And I am so happy to see you again."

They hugged each other and in the embrace, Alex started to get a little worried.

"Am I dead?" he asked her.

She smiled, "You are not dead, though I still am. We are in the realm that separates time from timelessness. It is the realm of the Chaos."

"I see. I've been attacked quite a few times, and imprisoned already. I can't say I'm a huge fan of this Chaos place."

"We are safe for now. I am able to feel his presence, and though he is technically in every molecule that is surrounding us, he is currently away. Where to, I am not sure."

"Who is this *he* you are referring to?"

"The King. Have you not met him?"

Alex shook his head and just stared at his mom, overcome with so many emotions that he could not find the words to express them.

"I take it that you were not aware that you were coming to meet me?" she broke the silence.

"No, I had no idea. Did you know?"

"Not at first, but eventually I did."

"There's so much I want to say to you Mom, so much I want to ask you that I don't even know where to start."

"Start anywhere. What would you like to talk about, Alex?"

"I don't know. I guess how I miss you and not a day goes by that I don't think about you. And Eric and Dad and Grandma – they all miss you too."

"I miss all of you as well."

"What's heaven like? Are Grandpa and Maggie there too?"

"It does not work that way. I am but a drop in the ocean of timelessness. There is no differentiating between the drop and the ocean itself."

"I see. So it's not all golden fields and sunshine and happiness all the time?"

"There is no need for any of that, I'm afraid. It is an immaterial, perpetual existence. Neither good nor bad. Those qualities have no place in heaven."

"That sounds kind of weird, actually. Do you like it?"

She shrugged as if to say that the question has no relevance, but did not want to sound too inhuman to her own son. Alex sort of caught the drift. There was no way he'd be able to grasp eternity. Somehow this focused his mind, though.

"Since you are here in front of me, Mom, there is something I've always wanted to say to you but never had the chance while you were still alive. Remember the day before I left for college, you mentioned seeing Adam Turner at the ice cream shop with his mom, and how you thought it would be nice for us to go get ice cream together before I left?"

"Of course," she said with a smile.

"But I had already made plans to go see my friend Luke, and I felt really bad about breaking them because he was moving to the UK the next day—"

Alex started crying, softly,

"—and you told me to go see Luke, and that you'd take a rain-check on the ice cream. I said I was only going there for a few hours, and that I'd make it home in time so that we could still get some. But I ended up getting too drunk with Luke, and I passed out. I never even called you to say I wasn't gonna make it, or to say that I was sorry,"

Alex paused for a second. Elizabeth kept on smiling, nodding in comprehension.

"Well, I'm sorry I didn't go get ice cream with you that day. I've always been sorry about it. Because—"

Alex could barely say the words.

"—because that opportunity never came up again, and I've never forgiven myself for it."

She looked at him with total compassion, and put her hand reassuringly on his face.

"But you must forgive yourself, Alex. You've always been far too hard on yourself."

"But I don't know what I was thinking, Mom. Maybe I was in disbelief that you were actually dying. Maybe it was because you had cancer for so many years, and so many procedures and operations had put it into remission for long periods at a time. Maybe I thought that was going to happen again, even though you and dad sat me and Eric down and told us that it had become terminal. There was finally nothing else the doctors could do. The cancer was just too strong. And I think part of me didn't believe it, even though I knew it to be true. I couldn't believe it. I didn't know how to believe it. And ever since then, I've always felt ashamed. I never stop thinking about that ice cream I should have had with you that day, and how Adam Turner, whose mother is and was perfectly healthy, got to have ice cream with her."

He broke down. She brought him in closer to her, and softly spoke,

"Please forgive yourself, my son. I forgave you the moment you left to see Luke. I remember being saddened by it at the time, but realizing that mothers and sons are meant to grow apart. Look at your relationship with your father, Alex. You both love each other very much, but there is a distance between you. It is only natural, and if I were still alive, we would have a distance between us, too. It is only because I am dead that you feel the need to be close to me. If I were still alive, you'd move on with your life with Stella, without me, though we'd still love each other. Like any other family, we'd talk on the phone every now and then, and see each other at holidays, but other than that, you'd have your own life. You only feel like there is unfinished business between us because we were not able to go through those stages naturally."

Alex looked at her, she was simply radiant against the backdrop of the Chaos.

"You know about Stella?"

"As I was held prisoner in this realm, your energy flowed through me, and that is how I knew of your arrival. Since you and Stella are eternally bound by blood, you are now one and the same source of energy. By virtue of being your mother, though, I was able to subtract her blood from what I knew was your blood, and in turn, understand Stella. And I am quite pleased with her, Alex."

"I'm glad to hear that. But will I ever get to see her again?

"I cannot see your fate, Alex, I am sorry. The future is a sphere within the sphere of time, and by my very nature, I am separated completely from time."

"I understand. How is it even possible that we are meeting here in the Chaos, though?"

"The blood oath that you and Stella made was the only oath that was ever powerful enough to cut through the Chaos and into eternity. The fact that my body and my blood were once again combined on earth inside of you, my direct offspring, via the mosquito that fed upon you, allowed us both——"

She cut herself off and looked concerned. "—the King is coming back. I can feel his energy regenerating around us. Remember this, son, that immortals cannot suffer pain. He has a sort of spell over me, and it may appear that I am in pain, but it is only the appearance of pain and nothing more. Don't let him fool you. He is all illusions. Nothing but smoke and mirrors and—"

And then the King of the Chaos materialized before their very eyes, and at these accusations, focused high-power streams of each element into Elizabeth's immortal being from every direction at once. She howled out in suffering.

"Only the *appearance* of pain?" he said in her direction. Alex charged at him, but Chaos held him off with a water force-field that he had placed in a circle immediately surrounding himself. Elizabeth was slowly fading as the elements pounded away at her. Alex banged at the force field but could not break through.

"You have a choice to make, human," Chaos said, as he shot an orb of liquid fire a few feet from Alex, thus ripping a portal into the dark matter. The portal spun and glowed very rapidly in the darkness.

"Walk through that portal and return to Earth, or stay here and watch your mother suffer the death after death. Nonexistence. And be stuck here with me for all of eternity."

"He lies, Alex. He does not have the power to do any of this."

Elizabeth shouted between agonizing screams. Chaos amped up the elemental attack on her, and she started disappearing more rapidly. Then he shot some more liquid fire into the glowing portal, causing an image of Stella to appear inside of it.

"Either you stay here and try to save your already doomed mother, or you return to Earth for your beloved Stella. But you cannot have both."

And with that, Chaos lowered his arms in a grand gesture and the portal started to shrink. 'You do not have much time, human. Who do you love more? Your mother or your lover? It's that simple."

Alex kept looking back and forth between Elizabeth and Stella. How could he decide between them? Ultimately life should win out over death, right? But what if his mother was right and this was all just illusions? What if he could save his mom and also return to Earth? He couldn't trust Chaos to return his mother to eternity if he decided to walk through the portal. But if he walked through, maybe everything would simply go back to normal, to how it was before all of this. Before the room inside the tunnel and the red-orange man with his glowing eye.

"Go to her!" Elizabeth shouted, as she was now just a thin filmy layer that was nearly gone. The portal was now the size of a quarter and he could no longer see Stella inside of it. "Before it's too late, son! Go!"

Chaos was laughing and it sounded like every atom of the dark matter was laughing with him. "Who do you love more, Alex, who do you love more?"

"I love you, mom," he finally said and ran as fast as he could into the portal. It closed behind him.

PART III: LOS ANGELES

XX

Alex opened his eyes. He was surrounded on all sides by a damp, charred-out wood. The smell of the wood was sweet to his senses. He stood up as well as he could, but his legs were slightly atrophied. As he steadied himself upon them, he looked out of a hole in the trunk that was located at his eye level. Through it he saw a magnificent sunlit forest of verdant redwood trees.

"Where am I?" He wondered.

When he thought about it some more, he realized that he didn't even know his own name, or who he was, or anything about himself at all. All he could remember before the present moment was nothingness. A giant blank. His memory was a complete void.

A few bluebirds on a tree somewhere in the distance could be heard, but other than that the forest seemed empty. He carefully crawled out. The giant redwoods stretched up to the clouds and continued out in every direction forever. A slight fog hung in the trees and it felt cool upon Alex's skin.

"Hello?" He cautiously proceeded through the forest on what appeared to be a walking path. No one responded. He continued on.

The sun was still high in the sky, so he reasoned that it had to be early afternoon or late morning. Just then, a barking dog could be heard further down the path. It sounded like it was getting closer to him. It was not long before an unleashed, shaggy white dog came running up to him and started sniffing his legs and ass.

"Maybe you could tell me what you find out," he said to the dog. Feeling a bit surreal, he went down and started sniffing the dog. It was friendly enough, wagging his tail and trying to lick Alex's face.

"Argos!" A woman was yelling from down the path. The slight breeze carried her echo through the trees as well. Suddenly it occurred to Alex that he had no clothes on. He was as naked as the dog and the trees of the forest. Even though he was sort of confused right now, he remembered enough about human nature to know that the woman who was approaching might not appreciate his nakedness. She might even scream and call the cops and what not. Since he didn't currently know anything about himself, he realized that he might have a hard time getting himself out of jail.

Alex quickly went to hide behind the nearest redwood, but his weakened legs gave up on him and he fell flat on his face. Had he fallen a few inches to the right, a branch that was sticking out of the ground would have made his fall a lot more painful.

Though all he could see from his vantage point was the ancient brown dirt of the forest, he heard the unmistakable laughter of the woman who had been approaching. He looked up and saw a girl whose eyes were sequoia brown, and whose hair swooped over her face, curly and golden in the sunlight. Her earthen perfume seemed to drizzle over him from above.

"What have you found here, boy?" She grabbed her dog by his collar and pulled him towards her. Not sure what to say, Alex just lied there silently with his ass in the air, figuring that was the better view.

"I'd like to believe that I don't have to call the cops on you, that you're just some one who partied a little too hard last night or something," she said, keeping a safe distance from him and placing her hand upon the cell phone in her purse just in case. The fact that she was speaking English reassured Alex that he was in America, or some place like America, like Canada or something.

"I'm, uh, sorry, ma'am. I'm not exactly sure how I got here, and uh, why I'm naked. Please do not call the cops on me. I promise you that I mean you no harm."

Argos barked at him. "Shush, dog," she chided him.

"It's okay, I guess. I mean, I suppose I believe you," she said. "Do you, um, need any help getting up? I don't mind the sight of a, um, uh, you know, if that's what you're worried about laying down there like that."

She sounded like somebody that could be trusted, given the current circumstances. Alex didn't really have much of a choice, anyways. Okay, I'll just pick myself up and try to play it cool, he thought to himself. As he turned around to face her, she did her best not to stare.

"Could you please tell me where I'm at?"

"Sure," she laughed a bit, "You're in the Armstrong National Forest of redwoods in Guerneville, CA."

"California?" he repeated. Huh?

"Not where you expected to be, I take it?" Alex shook his head.

"Where'd you think you were? Mars or something?"

"Yeah, something like that, I guess."

"You got a name?"

He shrugged.

"You don't know your name, even?" He just looked at her helplessly as she studied him over. "Curly. For now it's Curly, on account of your hair." He ran his fingers through his hair and supposed it had some curls in it.

"Okay," he agreed on the name. She stuck out her hand for a shake. He carefully extended his hand and shook hers.

"Hi Curly, I'm Candace. And I guess you already formally met Argos, the way you were sniffing at each other."

He smiled. "Yeah, we met. Nice to meet you Candace." She smiled back.

"If you don't even know your own name, I don't suppose you remember if you were with anybody else?"

"I'm sorry, I really don't know."

She looked him up and down. "If you plan on staying out here any longer looking like that, you're gonna end up in some kind of trouble. Why don't you come back to my place and see if we can't jog your memory a bit. I think I got some boy clothes at my place leftover from one of my exes."

"No, I couldn't put you out like that."

"But I insist. You're not exactly in any position to refuse my offer."

"True enough." He said, and did his best to cover himself on the way to her car.

XXI

Candace had a one-bedroom apartment that was set back three streets behind Guerneville's main street. At the town center was a two-room city hall-police station-post office combo, a bookstore, a local grocer, a few coffee shops ranging from basic to hip, a pizza place, a few bars, a small art gallery, a couple of novelty shops, a travel agency, a gazebo and benches for small gatherings and concerts, and a general small-town aesthetic that was conspicuously and proudly welcoming to alternative lifestyles of all natures.

Her apartment could be described as bohemian. It was not dirty, but rather a series of organized messes. There was no television and no computer, but there was a fairly sizable stereo system from a previous decade. There was one couch, a coffee table, a fish tank with three clownfish, and a corner that acted as her workspace for making the jewelry and ceramics and sculptures that were her true passion. Scattered about the apartment were finished pieces of her artwork, and in Alex's opinion, the pieces were all pretty good. The kitchen was a continuation of the main living room, and was narrow and confined by all definitions.

Her bedroom was just a bed and a dresser, and piles of clean and dirty clothes mixed together freely. It was gender-neutral by appearance, yet a hint of femininity somehow prevailed. The bathroom was the only other room in her apartment and it was clean enough, with only mild soap grime and stains that pre-dated Candace's residence upon the walls and shower.

When she brought the stranger from the forest back to her place, she said casually,

"Here it is. You can make yourself at home while you are here. I don't drink soda, so if you want that, it's on you. You have to hold the lever on the toilet bowl for five seconds before it will flush, and this couch you are staring at is your bed."

Alex, who was now wrapped in her father's Army blanket, took it all in. Argos found a corner of the room that the sun was shining in and plopped down comfortably.

"I really appreciate you taking me in like this, Candace. Naturally, I will find a job as soon as I can to save up and get out of your hair."

She clucked her tongue, "Nonsense, Curly. You've obviously been through something here. Just take your time getting back to normal, and then we'll talk about jobs and shit."

"Thanks. I owe you one."

They sort of studied each other for a moment, and then Candace added,

"I ain't gonna change my routine for you, though. I work at Moondog's Coffee in the center of town. Not today, but tomorrow I do. Right about now, if you weren't here, I'd smoke a little bit out of that bong over there," she motioned to a green glass bong sitting next to the coffee table, "and then I'd make myself a new necklace or something. You smoke?"

"Ummmm…" Alex thought about it, and of course, remembered nothing about his former life whatsoever. "I guess so. Why not?"

"Alrighty then."

She went over to the bong and picked it off the floor. It was still packed from a previous usage. She took a lighter off the coffee table and lit a rain-scented candle next to the couch, and then ripped the bong. She passed it to Alex and he took a hit.

Smoking marijuana was probably not the best idea for him. Candace had retreated into her workspace corner, and was stringing up glass beads with emeralds using great concentration. Alex was sitting on the couch and couldn't for the life of him figure out where to look. Everything he looked at filled him up with the deepest anxiety. The floor lamp was a little too narrow for the light that it was casting. The stereo system had a red blinking light that poked at his soul like a hot iron being thrust into it. Argos was panting so heavily and so rapidly that he wanted to massage him to sleep, but was not sure how Candace would take that. Would petting Argos be petting her by extension? Were they on that kind of level yet? He couldn't talk to or look at Candace because she did not seem to want any interruption. There might be some peace to be had in her bedroom, but how could he rightfully sit on her bed without it swallowing him up and spitting him clear out of the apartment?

Plus, he felt glued to the couch. Every time he tried getting up, one renegade cell in his body decided that it weighed a few tons and pushed him back down. He wanted to call somebody but he did not see a phone in her place. Also, he didn't know the number of anybody to call. His Mom? His Dad? That would be great, but who were those people? The police? Who would he tell them that he was?

71

He closed his eyes to try and sleep it off, but he could not fall asleep. All that happened when he did that was shut-eye hallucinations of himself on a rollercoaster with a skeleton as his passenger. It did not matter if his eyes were opened or if they were closed, he could find no comfortable state of being. He started to boil inside. He felt his blood bubbling up and the steam expanding his blood vessels. His skin tightened to contain it, but that just made his heart pound harder against his ribs. The organ beating against his bone made it hurt. It hurt so much that he had to let his skin go, and when he did, it popped. And when it popped, he screamed in pain.

Candace thought about coming over to help him, but decided to keep focusing on the bracelet she was making and let him work out his own demons. And they gnawed at him for several cold-sweat eternities.

It wasn't until sunrise of the next morning that he regained some semblance of composure. She was lying there on the couch next to him in an oversized T-shirt, spooned inside of him, and still he remembered nothing at all.

XXII

Alex lied awake on the couch for a while, taking a lot of comfort in having Candace close to him. He was not sure how she got there or if anything had happened between them, but her warm body calmed his, so he did not wake her.

She opened her eyes about twenty minutes later. Alex half-expected Candace to be surprised that she woke up next to him, but she was not. She kissed him on the cheek and got up. He was not sure how to ask her about the manner in which she ended up as his inside spoon. Candace could see that he was trying to figure it out and giggled a bit.

"We just fell asleep together, Curly. Nothing else. You were a perfect gentleman."

Her words relieved him.

"I see."

"Yup. Just some good-natured spooning," she reassured him. "I don't have any cool breakfast food, like ham and eggs or anything. But I got lots of cereal and oatmeal and stuff," she offered.

"Cereal sounds great," Alex said. "I remember how to make that, I think. I'll fix us up two bowls, if you'll let me."

She smiled. "It's in the cupboard. Knock yourself out."

She sat at the table and watched him as he prepared it.

"Anything come back to you?" she asked him.

He shook his head. "Not a thing."

"I'm sorry. I really am. It'll come back, though, sooner of later. I'm sure of it."

"You really think so?" he asked her. "What if I don't like who I am, though? What if I'm some chauvinist war criminal pedophile or something? I'll have to kill myself."

"Hush, Curly. You ain't any of those things. I can tell."

The cereal was ready.

***

"...And I miss the sunsets over the Mississippi the most. You could drink out in public on certain streets in Memphis, and nothing beats being a little buzzed as the old-style steam paddle-boats go up and down the river with the sun falling down behind them." She said with a faraway look in her eyes. They had been chatting over breakfast for hours now.

"Memphis sounds real nice, Candace," Alex said. "Why did you move here, then?"

"My friends and I camped up here a few years ago and I fell in love with it. I like it here, but I still miss home from time to time. You know?"

Alex nodded, though he had no comprehension of home.

"You got any family here?" he asked her.

"All back in Memphis." She answered. "It's just me and Argos, and those fish over there. And now you."

She gasped. She didn't mean to say it like that.

"Wow, you consider me family already?" he pressed the issue a bit.

"No, I mean, yeah, but no. You know, like I meant that you're here too. I mean, if I had to make some kind of Sophie's choice on whether it's you or the dog, Argos wins every time," she backpedaled as she blushed.

"Oh, okay," Alex laughed. "I see how it is." And before the tension could build to a point, she said,

"You should go check out the Russian River or one of the vineyards while I'm at the coffee shop. You can have my car. I walk to work, anyways."

"Maybe," he said. "Perhaps I'll just take Argos for a walk or something. Get a lay of the land."

Argos got up from the corner he had been in since getting back yesterday. Like any dog, he understood *that* word, and got excited. He went up to Alex and started jumping up on him.

"You shouldn't of said w-a-l-k around him. You just made him a promise, whether you realize it or not."

Alex pet the dog and said, "It would be my pleasure, Argos."

Candace got up from the table. "It's been nice talking with you, Curly, but I best be gettin' to work. You still gonna be here when I get back, or you plan on getting all naked inside a tree somewhere?"

He laughed. "No, I'll be here. I promise."

While she was at work, Alex took the dog for a walk and tried to prevent him from eating every blade of grass that he encountered along the way. When they got back, Alex sat on the couch and fell into the deep throes of a catnap.

He dreamed that he was an entire galaxy floating there in space, when suddenly another galaxy came crashing into him – destroying him into smithereens. Then he just hung there, as the smithereens. Scattered all over space.

XXIII

They went to the center of town around noon. Guys in dreads, and girls in dreads, and various other bohemian types of all ages had set up little stands around the gazebo area displaying their artwork. There were probably twenty artists there total, and Candace was one of them. She was selling necklaces made from gems and seashells and rocks. Alex was helping her keep track of what she sold and for how much.

There was a pretty healthy amount of people filtering through the art fair for a while, but things had started to slow down now.

"Since its slow, I'm gonna take a look around. That is, if you think you can handle being here alone," she said to him.

Alex brushed her off with his hand.

"Oh yeah, I'll be fine. Go take a stroll."

She smiled. "Thanks for your help today."

"My pleasure, Candace," he said and then she kissed him on the cheek and walked away.

Her kiss lingered on his cheek and then sunk into his skin like mercury. She had such soft, wonderful lips. He watched her walk away before a professor-looking guy in a corduroy jacket stepped up to the table and demanded Alex's attention with a clearing of his throat. He picked up the emerald bracelet that Alex had seen Candace make the first time he was at her apartment.

"This is very nice. How much do you want for it?" he asked.

Alex was a little reluctant to give it a price because of the memory he associated with it. It seemed crazy to him to sell away any kind of memory when he had so few of them.

"Ten bucks," he shrugged, and the professor seemed a little at-odds with the price.

"I see," the academic said, and thoughtfully stared at the bracelet. 'I'll give you eight."

"Sorry, no."

The professor gave it some serious consideration, then reached into his wallet and handed Alex the ten-dollar bill.

"You sir, drive a hard bargain," the man said, and walked away with the piece. Alex was sad to see the bracelet go.

About twenty minutes passed and Candace had still not come back. There was a blonde corporate hippy guy behind a tree that seemed to be staring directly at Alex. It was making Alex quite uncomfortable, so he tried his best not to acknowledge the fact that he was being spied on. Alex thought for a moment that he was just being paranoid, but when a few minutes went by and the guy was still there looking at him, he started feeling kind of nervous.

The stranger must have noticed that Alex had noticed him, and decided that the jig was up. Instead of peering at Alex from afar, he decided to approach him directly. Alex seriously considered running away from his stalker, but did not want to leave all of Candace's artwork out in the open like that. He held his post and confronted the stranger head-on, who was smirking as he approached the table.

"How in the hell did you get mixed up with all these gypsies, Alex?"

Was this guy talking to him? Was Alex *his* name?

"Sorry, man. I think you might have me confused with somebody else."

"Good one. Cut the crap, though."

"Do I know you? From where, if you don't mind me asking?"

"Are you for real, man?" He waved his hand over Alex's eyes to try and break the trance. "Earth to Alex. Earth to Alex."

"Why are you calling me Alex? Is that my name or something?"

"In general, I call people by their names," the stranger said. "Don't you...Alex?"

"I honestly don't remember ever meeting you. Sorry. I think I recently underwent some brain trauma or something."

John snapped his fingers in front of Alex's face violently.

"That snap you back to reality?"

Alex was starting to get frustrated, and feeling that he had no other form of recourse, clenched his teeth and balled his fist in order to defend himself. John noticed and put his arms up as if to surrender.

"Whoa, whoa, whoa, I don't want to fight you. It's John, dude. John, your manager. Remember?" He nodded in a patronizing way.

Alex lipped the words "manager" to himself in disbelief.

"Manager of what?" Alex asked.

"Are you trying to aggravate me, man? 'Cause it's working."

"Of course not. Are you trying to aggravate me?"

"Look, Alex, let's just get out of here. I'll explain everything to you on the way back to LA."

"No way, John. If that's really your name. I'll explain everything to you right now. I recently woke up naked in a redwood tree down the street, and before that, I remember nothing at all. Like seriously, nothing. God's truth."

John pulled out his cell phone.

"Yeah, I found him hawking shitty little necklaces at some gypsy hipster fair here in the center of town—"

"—Who are you calling?" Alex demanded. John signaled for him to hold on a minute.

"He's acting like he's got amnesia or some shit—"

"—I think I really do have it—"

"How should I know? Come see for yourself if he's faking it or not," John said and then he hung up.

"Who was that?" Alex insisted.

"Cliff. You know, the other guy we drove up the 5 with from LA. And then we all took that acid together, and it was crazy, and then all of a sudden you disappeared. And here you are, acting all absurd and shit."

"So I for sure live in LA?" Alex asked.

"You certainly do. And you better get your mind straight, 'cause you got that big meeting at William Morris in three days. In Hollywood, man. 'Cause you're a screenwriter," he said in the most condescending tone possible.

"William Morris? The talent agency?" Alex asked him, not sure how he could remember that but not his own name or personal history.

"Yeah, the talent agency, you big goofass."

Just then, Candace came back with a small painting of an angel on shale-rock.

"Hey Curly," she said, and then looked at John, not sure if he was a customer or not.

"And who might you be?" John asked her.

"I'm the artist, and this is my stand," she said with a hint of suspicion. "Can I help you?"

"Sure you can," John said, "What's he doing behind it?"

Candace glanced at Alex, and he shrugged.

"I'm not sure why that's any of your business," she said.

"And I'm not sure how it's not."

"You know this guy, Curly?" she asked Alex.

"Ummm—" Alex started.

"Curly? His name's Alex, hun,"

"*Alex?*" she looked over at him. "Is that really your name?"

Alex shrugged again. "He says he's my manager and that I'm a screenwriter from Los Angeles."

"And as much fun as all of this looks," John motioned flippantly to the festival, "I'm here to take him back to reality."

"He isn't going anywhere that he doesn't want to go,"

"Listen, honey, stay out of this and stick to selling your, um, art, to these local hicks and what not."

"I'm not going anywhere without Candace." Alex interjected.

"Sure, whatever. I don't care. Let her come."

"I'm not going anywhere with this neo-Nazi punk-ass."

"You're overstepping your bounds, patchouli girl."

"Hey man," Alex said, "don't talk to her like that."

"She's no longer allowed to come with us. And I don't care how good of a lay she is."

Candace threw one of her bracelets at him. He instinctually caught it.

"Thief!" Candace screamed. "This man is trying to steal my jewelry."

A gang of dreaded-thugs came out of nowhere towards John.

"Not cool, toots, not cool at all," he said as he quickly pulled his business card out and handed it to Alex,

"You better call me if you want to salvage your career as a screenwriter, bub," he said and then took off running before the tough-looking artists got any closer to him. The muscle followed after him as he hurried away down the street.

Da Bomb Group
John Sanderson
318 La Brea
Los Angeles, CA 90081
323-555-2031

Alex put the card in his pocket. He was a little confused by all of this.

"I swear that I've never seen that man before, Candace."

"I've seen all that I need to see of him."

They went back to Candace's place and smoked a joint while listening to surf music. Nothing more of John was said between them.

Later that night, they had sex for the first time. It was nice for both of them. They lost themselves completely within one another, and it was magical. But when it was done and they lay together in bed, Alex's mind couldn't help returning to John and the very real possibility that he was actually a Hollywood screenwriter.

XXIV

Candace woke up the next day as the sun rose through her bedroom window. She kissed a still asleep Alex on the back of his neck and breathed him in. She kissed him again in the same place and this time it woke him up.

Alex rolled over and stared into Candace's eyes.

"Good morning," he said to her.

She kissed him on his nose in response. "I gotta work in about an hour. After that, you wanna go see one of Sonoma's famed vineyards with me? It's very romantic, you know."

"That sounds wonderful."

"Good then, it's a date."

When she went to work, Alex quickly got bored just sitting on her couch waiting for her to get home. Argos politely suggested another walk, but Alex just wasn't feeling it. He pulled out the card he had placed in his pocket and stared at John's number. He didn't trust the guy too much, but his desire to learn more about his past life proved too strong.

Alex caved in and gave John a call. John was thrilled that Alex had contacted him, and they made plans to meet at the local Guerneville pizza joint to discuss matters further.

Alex got there before John did, and soaked in the mixture of Italian and Americana kitsch that served as the restaurant's theme. There was some local microbrews on tap, and Alex ordered one before he sat down at a table.

When John walked through the door, he was wearing shades and looked coked out of his mind. He smiled at Alex and kept his sunglasses on as he sat across from him.

"Hey there, buddy, glad you could make it," he said as rapidly as a semi-automatic. "You remember anything more, man? Anything at all? Like your birthday, or where you lost your virginity, or your favorite color or some shit?"

Alex shook his head. "Sorry John, not a thing."

John sighed and pulled out a cigarette. He managed to light it and draw a deep inhale before the red-haired waitress came over to the table.

"You can't smoke that in here," she said, politely. "I'd be happy to get you a drink though, hun," she said as she put her hand on his wrist playfully. John put his cigarette out on the table. "I'll take your best tequila with a lemon, toots." She winked at him and disappeared.

"Why'd she wink at you like that?" Alex wondered out loud.

"My big fuckin' cock, man. Chicks can smell it," he said, but then quickly changed the subject to, "Seriously though, you're coming to LA if I have to slip you a fuckin' roofie, you stubborn, amnesiac fuck."

"Settle down man. Let's get down to business. What's with this big meeting I supposedly have in a few days?"

"I thought I explained it to you a hundred times already, but I guess I'll say it again. You have been contracted to write the sequel to *Gone with the Wind* over at MGM, and we're talking big bucks here man. Since you don't remember, we're coming hot off the heels of your motherfuckin' Oscar-nominated black comedy drama

84

whatever the fuck it was about your mother's bout with cancer—"

"Shut up, man!" Alex interjected. Suddenly a flash of memory hit him. His mother, pale and emaciated from the endless rounds of chemotherapy and surgeries she went through to try and stay alive for him and his brother. Holy shit, he had a brother. What was his name, though? What else did he have?

"What did you say about my mother?" Alex asked him.

"Huh? Nothing. Just that you wrote the movie about her, in her honor."

"In her honor? So, she is dead, then?"

This was not a very comfortable conversation for John to be having.

"I believe so, yes. Sorry, I mean, all I know is from what's in the screenplay. I didn't like personally know her or anything."

Alex was saddened by this, but much to his surprise, not surprised by it.

"How about the rest of my family? Do you know any of them?" he wondered.

"Can't say that I do. I never met any of them, and you never really spoke much about them. Now about the direction that the suits want you to approach the sequel from—"

"—Wait, but you must at least know my last name if you're my manager. Right? I could track the rest of my family down on the internet or something and—"

"—Uh, I wouldn't be so sure of that."

"How do you not know my last name?"

"To me you're Alex Logan, but um, that's a stage name, man."

"A stage name? For a writer?"

"Yeah, it's Hollywood. Everyone's got a stage name. PA's got stage names. Your real last name is some kind of Eastern European impossible to pronounce, mouth-full-of marbles shit. It was changed before I ever met you."

"Then who would know it?"

John shrugged.

"How do I know beyond a shadow of a doubt that I actually know you at all?" Alex asked him.

"That's a good question," he said as he scrolled through his smart phone. "I'm sure I got a picture of us somewhere in here. Ah! Here we go." He handed Alex his phone. There was a picture of him and John with sombreros on next to a couple of girls at a bar. Alex studied the picture.

"Who are they?"

"Hell if I know. Some blondes that didn't stick around for long."

Alex had more questions for him. A lot more questions, but did not know where to start. He stood up at the table.

"Look, I need some more time with all of this. I'm going back to Candace's to think on it. I'll call you in a few days."

John stood up as Alex was leaving,

"Fine, fuck *Gone with the Wind 2* for a minute, but your home is in LA, man. Your fuckin' home. You gotta remember to at least pay the rent. It's already the 27th."

The waitress brought John his tequila, a lemon, and her phone number. He shot it down without the need for the lemon or the number. Something John said had stopped Alex dead in his tracks. It was the word "home." Alex walked back to the table and sat down.

"Where in LA do I live?" he asked John, who was all-too pleased to answer.

"In West Hollywood," he said. "Between Melrose and Beverly. A little east of La Cienega. On a street called Croft."

"Do I have any roommates or anything?"

"Nope."

"And no family in LA?"

"Jesus, Alex. No, none that I know of. But who knows. Maybe some distant cousin I never met or some shit."

Hmmm, that was interesting to hear. Maybe Candace would go there with him so that he did not have to investigate this all on his own. He vaguely recalled Candace saying that she hated LA, though.

"How many bedrooms?" he asked John.

"None. It's a studio. You told me you don't need any bedrooms. Just a place to write. I said you should have some bedrooms, but you disagreed."

"Okay," Alex said, admitting a sort of defeat. "I guess I want to see it. I'll have to think about this whole *Gone With the Wind 2* business, though."

"What's there to think about? They want to give you a million bucks to write it. Writers aren't even supposed to make that kind of money."

"That is a lot of money. I just don't know if I could even write a paragraph in my current state of mind," Alex admitted.

"Fuck your state of mind. You'll snap out of it. I promise. This kind of thing happened to Billy Wilder all the time. We leave tomorrow, though. I gotta be back in LA for one of my other clients."

"Okay. I'll call you tomorrow when I'm ready."

XXV

Later in the afternoon, Candace took Alex to the vineyards of the lush Dry Creek Valley of Sonoma County. They went to a couple of tastings and walked the grounds of some of the more lavish estates.

There was a charming little café located at the one estate, and they dined there and talked about nothing in particular. Alex and Candace got along very well, and they even had similar senses of humor. So it was hardly a surprise when they got back to Candace's place in the evening that she said to him,

"I love you, Alex," after they had lazily drunken sex together on her bed. He let the words sink in. He didn't know what to say to her, so he said nothing at all. It broke his heart to stay silent, though, seeing her exposed and vulnerable for the first time since he had known her. He shed a tear that he did not let her see, and remained silent for a moment longer. That moment, though, was all she needed to understand that she had miscalculated. She looked away from him, rolled off the bed, and walked away naked. She picked up her pink, silk robe on the way out of the room.

Goddammit, he thought to himself. He should have said something, anything. She had taken him in, fed him, stimulated his mind, given her body to him without question, and he said nothing?

Truth be told, part of him did love her. Part of him was itching to look even deeper into her brown eyes than she looked into his, grab her body with both of his arms and pull her in closer to tell her that he loved her too, that he had always loved her. But something was stopping him. He was not sure what it was, but it was for sure something. However small that shred of whatever it was may be, it was standing in the way, and he just could not respond to her.

The regret that he felt filled his body and increased in waves as the seconds passed. Even if he went running after her to wherever she had gone, he could not make this right. There was no way to take back his hesitation. Even if they got together and made up, that hesitation that had come between them would grow over time and eventually destroy them. He decided to go after her anyways.

She hadn't gone too far. She was in the other room with her head buried into the couch, sobbing lightly. He sat down next to her and she did not fight it. He wasn't even sure if she knew if he was there or not. Her sadness was really getting to him, though, so he put his right hand on her back to try and comfort her in some way. She immediately twisted off of the couch, onto the floor,

"Don't you touch me. Don't you ever touch me again."

"I'm sorry," he said. And he truly was.

"Just get out, Alex. Get the fuck out of here."

And then she collapsed completely onto the hardwood floor, and he stared at her convulsing body from the couch. She looked so beautiful in her sadness, so utterly Victorian.

"Please don't make me leave. You just caught me off guard. I am sorry, Candace. I want to tell you that I love you, too, and maybe I do. Lord knows that you've been so good to me. But we've only known each other for a few days now. How could either of us know we are truly in love with each other? Maybe I do love you, I'm not sure, but I think it's just too soon to tell. I don't want to lie to you or hurt you in the long run."

She sniffled a bit and wiped her nose with her robe. Then she turned around and said,

"I know for sure, Alex. I knew from the moment I saw you that I loved you."

Alex was not sure if that was entirely possible, but he believed that she thought it was.

"Look Candace, I'm still really confused. I don't even know who I am, really, or where I came from. I'm not sure I can commit to anything before I know for sure. For my sake, and for your sake. Maybe we should have never confused our relationship by having sex. But we did, and maybe we just shouldn't have so soon."

She just shook her head and buried her head back in the couch. Alex couldn't take it any longer. "I'm gonna leave, Candace, like you want me to. I won't cause you any more problems," he said as he got up and headed for the door. "Thanks for everything," he said and turned the knob on the door to open it. As soon as he started stepping out, he heard her say quietly, but loud enough for him to hear,

"I'll kill myself if you leave."

XXVI

After giving Alex only a day to think about if he wanted to go back to LA or not, John was at Candace's door, calling on him. Alex was not sure how John found the place, but figured that he had his ways. Candace was working the early shift at the coffee shop, so Alex was alone. He did not open the door right away, so John knocked on the door a little harder.

"Open up, Alex, I know you're in there. I can hear you breathing through the door."

Really? That's kind of impressive actually, Alex thought. He was all set to leave with John, but then last night's episode with Candace was giving him doubts about going to LA. He did not want her to make good on her threat and kill herself if he went. He couldn't deal with the blood on his hands. He would need a few more days to think it all over. John would just have to understand.

He took a deep breath and then opened the door. John was there by himself in hipster regalia, dark-rimmed glasses and all.

"Good morning, John," Alex said to him and let him inside.

"You know for most writers in Hollywood, the exact opposite is going on. They're beating my door down."

Alex shrugged, "Yeah, well, I guess I'm one of the lucky ones."

John looked around Candace's place to survey the scene, "So this is the palace that you've been so reluctant to leave," he said wryly, as he motioned to a pile of dirty clothes collecting in the corner. "I mean, its got some lower caste kind of charm, I guess."

Alex chose to ignore the insult.

"So are you ready to go or not?" John asked. "You don't look ready. Are you even packed yet?"

"Yeah, about that—" Alex started.

John pounded the cluttered coffee table with his fist.

"I knew it! I fucking knew it! What the fuck am I gonna tell Howard, huh? He thinks you're already on-board."

"Who's Howard?"

"What, are you fucking sniffing glue over here? He's your agent, Alex. Howard's been your agent for years now."

"Then why isn't he bothering me, too?"

"Well if your head was right, you might remember how he does not like to micro-manage. I mean, he put this shit together for you, made you part of the package. Now it's on me to get you to say yes. As far as he's concerned, though, you're already on board. That's what I told him. That's why he's not calling you. He thinks you're doing it, and that we just came up here to clear your head before you started writing it."

"I don't even know this Howard guy. I don't even know you, John. This is getting ridiculous," Alex said.

"You're telling me? My best client is shit-for-brains all of a sudden after one bad acid trip, shacked up with some barista chick, and unresponsive to financial gain. Don't you want to move out of your Weho studio apartment?"

"Weho?"

"Yeah, West Hollywood. Where you live. For the last time, ass."

Alex stared at him blankly. He felt like a crazy person.

"You obviously have no fucking clue what I'm talking about."

They just stood there looking at each other.

"Can you at least get me some fucking coffee or liquor, or something? Or did you forget what those things are too?"

"Yeah, sure," Alex said and went into the kitchen. There was still some coffee on the pot, and he poured it out for them into mugs. He put a little whiskey in there too. He walked back into the other room and set it down on the coffee table.

"Thanks," John said, and tasted it. The whiskey made him wince a little bit, but he took some more.

"I've got to use the bathroom," Alex informed him and headed down the hallway. He wondered what he could tell John to buy a little more time.

In the bathroom, Alex looked at himself in the mirror to try and find himself deep down somewhere in his own reflection. He resolved to stay in Guerneville for now, and tell John that he just had to deal with it.

When he came back, he sat on the floor across from John and took a few sips of his coffee.

"Look John, I do believe that you have my best intentions in mind, but there are things here that you are not privy to that I can't just run away from."

"Like what? All of this?" He motioned once more around the room, mockingly.

"She told me that if I left she would kill herself, okay? I don't want that to happen. I need to talk with her a little more, and in a few days—" but then blackness washed over Alex, and he fell towards the floor. Before his head hit the hardwood tile, though, John caught him.

"Can't have you hitting your head and doing any more damage to it, can we now?"

And then he dragged Alex away and placed him in the backseat of the car that was waiting for him out front. Cliff was in the driver's seat and started it up.

"Let's get this crazy-ass back to LA." John told him.

Cliff, who was more or less just some average guy from Southern California, said,

"I wish it didn't have to come to this."

"Me too," John said. And then they were off.

XXVII

Alex woke up alone in a studio apartment efficiency. It was sparsely furnished, with only a photograph of a tractor taken during the magic hour hanging on the otherwise blank beige walls of the ultra-small confines.

He walked out onto the patio that was connected to the room, and admired a clear view of the Hollywood Sign to the north. That was when he realized that he was in Los Angeles, and that this must be *his* apartment. Immediately outside his window were palm trees and red honeysuckles that hummingbirds fed upon. A power line ran overhead across the span of the apartment complex, and a squirrel was using it as his own personal highway through West Hollywood.

The last thing he remembered was talking to John at Candace's place, and now he was here. The only reasonable explanation for how he got here was that John drugged him, as he had promised, and forced him here. What was he going to tell Candace? He couldn't stand the idea of her killing herself because John took matters into his own hands.

He spied a rotary phone sitting in a corner on the floor. When he picked up the phone and heard the dial tone, he realized he did not know her phone number. For that matter, he did not know any phone numbers. As far as he knew, he had no cell phone, and even if he did, she would not be in it.

He went to the computer to try and look her number up. When he typed 'Candace' into Google, he realized that he didn't even know her last name. He never had. He typed in 'Guerneville Candace' but nothing came up. He paced the room out of frustration.

It was not long before he remembered that she worked at Moondog's Cafe. He searched for it and wrote the phone number down on a scrap piece of paper, and then was going to head for the phone when a folder on his computer desktop labeled *screenplays* caught his eye.

He opened the *screenplays* folder. There were four finished screenplays there. One was a fairy tale about a princess and a penguin who had to save the day from a dark sorcerer named Toledo; one was a stoner-western comedy set during the Mexican Revolution; one was a comedy about a guy working at a pizza shop that secretly fought aliens, and the last one was about some guy with the same name as him working in national security and getting wrongfully accused of being the mastermind of some terrorist plot set during the World Series. Alex had no recollection of writing any of these, but sure enough, there was his name on each and every one of them. They had all been registered with the guild, even. He saw no signs of *Gone with the Wind 2* or that Oscar-nominated one John had mentioned.

He was hungry, so he went to his fridge. All he found in it were a couple of eggs and some almond milk. Not very appetizing. He opened the freezer. It too was sparse, with only a frozen pizza and a half-filled bottle of tequila. He took out the tequila and noticed that he had some lemons on the counter, fresh enough to not be considered rotten. He found a shot glass in his cupboards and filled it with the cold tequila. He cut up the lemon and grabbed a shaker of salt that was sitting further down the counter. He poured some on his hand, downed the shot, and then took the lemon to his face. He repeated this several times.

In his drunken state, he decided to look more carefully around his small apartment. He first sought out to find some evidence of his family. Some pictures or something. Anything really. But alas, he found nothing of the sort. He did find some film theory books, most of them containing French New Wave criticism, and also found a prescription bottle under the sink. Inside of its orange walls was about an eighth of marijuana. On the bottle it said that it was only to be used for medical purposes, under the laws of the State of California, Proposition 215. The weed had a name – *Trainwreck*.

Close by, he found a green and yellow turquoise pipe that he stuffed the pot into. He grabbed the lighter next to the bottle and toked that shit up. It was like ice-crystals had entered his lungs and then decided to stay there and party. He was messed up, to say the least. Super-stoned. At that moment, his phone started ringing and on the caller ID it said *Gavin*. Who was that? Because of his current level of intoxication, his curiosity won out and he picked up the phone.

"Hello," he slurred out.

"Yo Alex, what up?" the deep voice on the other end said, pronouncing the "a" in Alex's name more like an "o," but not quite as harshly.

"Um, I'm pretty drunk, man," he said and then added, "and, uh, stoned, too." Gavin laughed on the other end of the call, "Yeah, me too. You want to come down to Pedro and chill?"

"Pedro?" Alex said, totally clueless.

"Yeah, you know, San Pedro."

Alex was not sure how to play this one. Clearly he did have a life here, and there were people other than John who knew him. He just didn't know any of them.

"Dude, Gavin," he was improvising, "I don't know how to say this, and please don't get offended, but—"

"—But what man?" his tone changed into one of concern. "Is everything okay over there?" The sincerity caught Alex a little off-guard.

"Yeah, everything's great, except, I mean, I feel totally crazy about this because I know I've been there like a zillion times before, but I forgot where you live exactly."

Gavin told him the address.

"Sober up and then type that shit into google maps, man," he said, completely understanding of Alex's current predicament. Even though he thought it was somewhat ridiculous, there was no sense of judgment in his voice.

"So you comin' down then?" he asked him.

"Yeah, I'll see you in as long as it takes me to get there."

XXVIII

Right before Alex was about to head out the door down to San Pedro, the scrap of paper that had the number to Moondog's caught his eye from the desk. Somehow, he had totally forgotten about it. He didn't know how to explain why he was in LA, but he owed it to her to at least call her.

He dialed the number and let it ring a moment, breathing heavily into the receiver.

"Thank you for calling Moondog's Cafe, Leliza speaking."

"Um, hi, Leliza. Is Candace there?"

She did not respond to him directly, but he heard her call out to Candace, "Yo Candy, it's for you."

"Who is it?" he heard Candace ask.

"I don't know girl, just answer the damn thing," Leliza shot back at her. A moment passed and then Candace picked it up.

"This is Candace," she said.

"Hey, it's Alex."

"Where you at, Curly? You just up and leave me like that?" she was pissed.

"No, no, honestly I didn't. John drugged me and dragged me to LA. I'm in my West Hollywood apartment."

"He drugged you?" she asked.

"I believe so, yes."

"And you're in Los Angeles, like, for real?"

"For real," Alex replied.

"Are you coming back here at all?"

"I don't have any way of getting back there."

"Don't you have a car?"

"I don't know. That's a good question. I'm actually not really sure if I have a car or not. I'll have to look into that."

"Buy a bus ticket if you don't," she suggested.

"I don't have any money, though," Alex confessed.

"Damn," Candace said and there was silence for a moment. "I thought your crazy ass was in jail or something. But you're in LA, huh?"

"Yep. My apartment here is about the *size* of a jail cell." Alex tried joking. She wasn't really having it, though.

"So you're staying down there, then?"

"Looks like it. It does seem like I actually live here. Figured it might be easier to sort things out from home."

"I could wire you money for the bus ticket," Candace offered.

Alex thought about it for a second, "I think I better stay here for a while."

More silence. Alex could sense tears forming in her dark, wonderful eyes. He did not want to make her sad.

"You can come live with me if you want, Candace. I'd really like it if you did that."

She sniffled a bit. "I fucking hate LA."

"Come here just for a while then. You don't have to stay if you don't want to."

"What about the coffee shop?" she asked. "I gotta work the next week straight."

"I don't know," Alex said, "Fuck the coffee shop."

Candace paused. "I gotta think about it, Alex,"

"Okay," he said, but she had already hung up.

XXIX

Alex searched every nook and cranny of his place and managed to find a set of car keys lying underneath some notebooks. He did have a car, then. That was good news.

He made his way down into the garage of the apartment complex and went to the space that corresponded with his apartment number. Sure enough, there was a little silver coupe sitting there, dirty from all the endless barrage of LA sunshine and smog. He tried the key in the door and it worked. He put the directions he had printed out on the passenger seat.

He went a couple of miles down La Cienega and watched it turn from the glamour of Beverly Hills to the relative squalor of Culver City. There was a billboard set up every five feet along the two-mile stretch of road. The advertisements somehow managed to pick up in frequency as he took the exit for the 10 freeway and headed east towards downtown. To the left of him, in the distance, he could again see the Hollywood Sign and the famous hills that surrounded it. The road itself was dirty and busy, but he was certainly enjoying all of the palm trees.

On the harbor freeway, he was utterly fascinated by the thousands of massive concrete bridges that rose up and across the sky before him in a futuristic tableau. It was like a symphony of infrastructure that gradually segued into a steady lull of industrial buildings and factories. There were less palm trees down this way and a lot less traffic, but noxious vapors from the countless chemical plants abounded.

When he got down alongside the port itself, he was amazed by the endless lines of giant cranes, the millions of smokes stacks, the long docks with their multicolored containers of cargo stacked up to the heavens, and the humongous ships and freighters coming in and going out of the harbor. Connecting everything was a long blue suspension bridge that cut along the coast to a place called Terminal Island, and then from there over to Long Beach, which was currently hiding behind a curtain of pollution. On the island, fires burned in factories the size of theme parks, and each flame reflected off of the ocean below it in an overwhelming chorus of commerce. The scale of the port impressed Alex so much, that he almost crashed his car as the speed limit drastically dropped where the freeway officially ended into a normal street that led right into the heart of San Pedro.

Off the exit, he was at Gavin's place before he knew it. He lived in a small ranch with aluminum siding, a little lawn, and a mirror ball decoration that rested just below his barred-off front window.

When Alex knocked on the door, a tattooed-up ex-Marine answered it with his shirt off, looking very muscular and imposing, yet friendly.

"What's up, man?" He asked as he let Alex into his home.

"I don't really know, but I think I've got amnesia."

"You were fine the last time that I saw you. A little stoned, maybe, but fine. What happened?" Gavin asked him.

"Beats me. When was it that you saw me last?" Alex wondered.

"Weeks ago, maybe. You were about to head up to wine country with your manager and shit. Did you ever do that?"

"Yeah, but, um, I mean, I don't remember anything before the point that I woke up naked in a redwood tree. Some chick named Candace found me there and I've been living with her for a while. Today I mysteriously woke up in my West Hollywood apartment."

"Damn, dude. That's messed up. Does this Candace chick got some big titties?"

"Yeah, I guess,"

"So you, uh, fucked her, then?" Gavin asked.

"Well…yeah."

Gavin nodded in approval. "Nice."

Alex scanned Gavin's place over and could tell from all the plaques and medals that Gavin had quite the accomplished military career. There was a giant porcelain cat on the coffee table, and the TV was on with the volume turned low. From the scattered notebooks and the open laptop it appeared that he was writing something before Alex got there.

"You want a brew?" He offered.

"Sure."

Gavin led him into the little kitchen and handed him a beer.

"You down to do some fishin' today?" he asked Alex.

"Yeah. That sounds good to me."

"Cool. I gotta go take care of something first, though."

Alex waited in the kitchen, as Gavin disappeared into his backyard. Through the windows, Alex could hear the sound of wood breaking, and then what sounded like marbles being spilled out onto concrete. After a few seconds of silence, Gavin came back inside.

"Alright man, let's go."

They took the short walk over from Gavin's house to Point Fermin Park on the coast. There was an old lighthouse there that the park had been built around, but was no longer functional. Along the edge of the park there was a stone fence, and beyond it was the endless brilliance of the Pacific Ocean. On the horizon, shrouded in mist, was Catalina Island, and apparently on very clear days it was possible to see parts of the Mexican coastline to the south.

At one end of the park was an amphitheater that the city of San Pedro had built back in the 70s, which was now being utilized by a little boy and girl who were playing hopscotch on the stage. At the other end of the park was the Korean Bell, a very large, colorful bell that Korea had donated in the name of friendship early on in the 20th century. The sun was out, as it always was in LA, and there was a very soft breeze that carried the ocean with it. The unmistakable aroma of the world's third busiest port mixed in with the ocean air, but the park was situated upon the bluffs in such a way as to block out the view of the port itself.

Over the stone fence at the park's perimeter were jagged precipices that led about a hundred feet down toward the ocean. Gavin hopped over the fence and Alex followed. They carefully walked along a very narrow ledge towards a more hidden fence. This one was made of metal and blocked off access to a region known as Sunken City. Somebody had dug a hole underneath the fence that was just big enough to squeeze under, so that's exactly what they did.

Sunken City was an embankment on the Pacific's Coast located between Point Fermin and the port. There used to be a military base at Sunken City, but it had fallen into the ocean decades ago. There were still huge pieces of road and debris that had been left there from when the base collapsed and was never cleaned up. Graffiti artists did their thing on the crumbled sections of the asphalt that still remained intact. Beer cans, condom wrappers, shopping carts and wild fennel were scattered throughout the ancient ruins. From there, rock mounds led down to the ocean's pebbly shore, but he and Gavin stayed on the high ground.

Gavin led Alex over the mounds of broken concrete and limestone with an adeptness befitting his military training. Finally they came to an area with a ledge not big enough for even half of Alex's foot. If he fell off of it, there was a gathering of cacti beneath him that would surely end in his death or needle-filled paralysis.

Gavin gracefully slid across the ledge and waited for Alex, who had to first gather his composure. He took a deep breath and crossed much more easily than he thought was possible. He thus passed the most treacherous stretch of their mini-journey. The path down to the cave wasn't too bad, though he did scratch his right knee on some bramble. At the sight of the blood, Gavin said,

"Keep that blood in the boat or the sharks'll surround us."

"Sharks?" Alex asked.

"Sure. Lots of hammerheads around these parts. Great whites, too."

"Well, that's terrifying."

"You'll be fine," he reassured Alex and ripped a portion of his sleeve off, "Just tie this around it, man." He did as he was told.

It was not long before they were upon the sea cave. Alex thought that it looked every bit as magical as any sea cave ought to look, all covered in barnacles, seaweed and anemone. It was deep, too. Gavin had shoved the boat back far enough into it to avoid the attention of any random passersby. He hid it in such a dark corner that even if a person was in the cave, they would surely have no idea that it was even there.

**

They had been out on the water for about an hour or so. Neither one of them had caught any fish, but it didn't really matter. The waters were calm and the sun was hot and invigorating. The coldness of the Pacific kept everything comfortable. The water was hypnotic, and under its spell, Alex felt relaxed for the first time in a while.

"So this other day I was at the strip club, right?" Gavin started off.

"Okay."

"And I was just sitting there drinking a beer with my one buddy, when this hot chick came up to me and just started giving me a lapdance."

"For free?" Alex asked.

"Yeah, for free. And she was hot, man. Like real hot. And you know how you're not supposed to touch the strippers and all that shit?"

Alex nodded.

"Well this chick was taking my hands and putting them all up in her tits and stuff. It was crazy."

"Wow."

"Yeah, but then," he continued, "Then she took my hand and reached it around her crotch, right, and like, she had balls, man."

"Really?" Alex asked him, genuinely surprised by the twist of his story.

Gavin nodded. "Yeah, it was pretty weird."

"Huh," Alex grunted and laughed.

Then they sat there and fished for a while in silence. Alex thought he caught something, but it was just a clump of seaweed. They opened up fresh beers and then sparked a joint that Gavin had brought.

"So I was wondering," Alex began, "Do you know anything at all about my background, like where I'm from, or anything about my family?" he asked as he passed the joint.

"You've never really mentioned anything like that to me before. I mean, you're a pretty private guy, Alex. Reclusive, even. And that's coming from a vet."

"Of course I am," Alex said as he exhaled out some frustration. "Any ideas on other friends of mine who might know the answers to those questions?"

He shook his head.

"Sorry, man. If you got other friends, I've never met 'em."

"I see," he said, clearly disappointed.

"I know this is easy for me to say," Gavin started as he inhaled, "but try not to worry about it. I think you'll snap out of this shit before too long."

"Yeah, you're probably right. Thanks, man."

And they fished and got more intoxicated. Alex learned nothing more of himself, but was happy to see that he had at least one true friend in Los Angeles.

XXX

Alex and John pulled into a parking garage underneath one of the two identical towers that stood in the center of Century City. The garage was filled beyond capacity with smog and it bothered Alex's sinuses. After John parked his yellow sports car, they took an elevator up towards the lobby. He had agreed to write *Gone With The Wind 2*, at least tentatively. He figured he was already in LA and did in fact appear to be a screenwriter. He also figured that the million dollar paycheck he would supposedly earn might help him towards finding things out about his past.

"It was totally uncool of you to drug and kidnap me like that, by the way," Alex said to him.

John laughed as the elevator doors opened, "Any good manager would have done the same thing in my position."

They entered the expansively ornate lobby. Everything was made of crystals and gold. The security guard standing at the marble front desk stopped them.

"Names? And who are you two trying to see?" he asked evenly.

"John Sanderson and Alex Logan, here to see Howard Kleinman," John said. The guard looked it up on his computer, picked up the phone and said something into it. When he hung up he said,

"Wear these," and handed them visitor passes to clip onto their shirts. They walked back to the elevators and went up towards the fourth floor.

"Lets try to act a little calmer than the last time you were here," he said to Alex.

"I don't remember ever being here," he reminded John.

"Oh yeah, that shit again. Well these cats are gonna look at you like you're nuts if you say that. Especially since you were here with me less than a month ago. You wore that same half-ass shirt that you're wearing now, actually."

Alex examined his wardrobe.

"This is a nice shirt, man."

They got off on the fourth floor and checked in with the secretary at the front desk. She was blonde and attractive and as cold as tungsten. She knew who they were and picked up the phone without verbally acknowledging them. When she hung up, she motioned for them to sit in the lobby.

The lobby was kind of boring, but it did have a superfluous amount of modern structure-paintings abounding on the walls and the floor. To each side of the couch were long windowless hallways with desks placed every ten feet apart from one other. Guys and girls in slick suits wore headpieces at each desk, and they were all typing away furiously on their keyboards and talking just as fiercely into their headsets.

Alex and John were waiting next to a bizarre Brazilian man in a dark blue suit and a redheaded vixen that Alex vaguely recognized from the supermarket tabloids he saw on his way to buy more tequila the day before. In a few moments, the elevators opened and a sharply dressed Asian man approached them.

"Follow me, gentlemen. Mr. Kleinman is ready to see you."

He took them back into the elevators, turned a key into the switchboard and then entered a code into it. They silently went up three floors. Then they walked out into a hallway that had more desks on the right side of the room, and a series of window offices on the left. The people at the desks to the right were sitting at slightly better desks than the ones three floors below them, and their desks were an additional ten feet apart from one another. They worked just as hard.

Halfway down the hallway, they were passed off to a young corporate woman that led them to the third last window office on the left. A middle-aged man starting to grey a bit, who looked like he could have been a linebacker in a previous lifetime, was sitting at his spacious desk in his spacious window office. He motioned to her to let them inside. First she asked them if she could get them anything to drink.

"Club soda, dear," John said.

"Yeah, club soda for me too," Alex said.

When she opened the door, the big man stood up to greet them from behind his desk.

"How's my favorite writer doing?" he asked as he extended his hand for a shake.

"Alright, I suppose. And you?" Alex asked him as naturally as he could.

"Just peachy keen. And nice to see you again, John."

John nodded back to him, "And you, Howard."

The assistant brought them some French sparkling water.

"Thanks hun," Howard said to her with a wink. "So today's the day all your dreams finally come true, Alex. You get to sign a deal that will let you move up in this town from looking at the hills to living in the hills," he laughed at his own cleverness.

"I kind of like my place," Alex told him.

"Sure you do," Howard said, "I, uh, apologize. The MGM guys got stuck on PCH but are on their way."

"No problem at all, Howard," John said. Howard sort of glared at him as if he had talked out of turn, then asked Alex,

"So maybe you wanna run through your final pitch a bit with me first?"

Alex felt his heart drop through the floor down into the smoggy parking garage. He suddenly could not breathe very well. Howard and John were both staring at him in anticipation. With his head feeling like it was in a vice, Alex tried playing it cool,

"John didn't tell me that I needed to have one prepared for today," he responded.

Howard laughed once and then got serious. "That's a good one. But seriously, let's hear it."

John was starting to squirm in his chair a little bit.

"Come on Alex, you knew you had to pitch today," he tried to say jokingly.

Alex looked back and forth between them.

"No, I didn't," he replied very quietly.

"You've been at this for years now, kid. You knew that you needed a pitch before the producers sign on. Tell me you're joking."

"I'm sorry Howard, but I'm not joking. I, uh—"

Howard screwed his face up.

"—This really isn't funny anymore, Alex," John cut in.

"What isn't funny anymore?" Howard demanded.

"Nothing's funny, sir. Nothing's ever been funny. I just think that I have amnesia and—"

"You fall off a fuckin' horse or something?"

"No, I uh, don't know what happened, but I guess I just thought that if I was around familiar surroundings that things would come back to me. I figured all I had to do was sign some contract or something. I mean, I have some vague recollection of having wanted to become a famous Hollywood screenwriter, but other than that—"

"—You *are* a famous Hollywood screenwriter. And let me tell you, this is you fucking it up," Howard said.

Then he focused his attention on John.

"Look, Johnny boy, I don't know what's going on with your client, but you better jog his memory before they get here. Now, I've got a phone call to make to a sane person, so why don't you two step out of my office and come back in when you start making sense."

"But he's your client, too, Howard," But Howard just waved him off and started talking into his phone.

John turned to Alex.

"You're making us both look stupid here," and then he grabbed him and led him into the hallway. "You're not indispensable on this project, Alex. Howard can just kick it to one of his other clients in a snap, if that's not what he's already doing."

Alex was nothing if not frustrated. "Sorry man, I tried being honest in there with both of you, but you won't believe me. What else can I do?"

"Sudden onset amnesia is not a fucking thing."

114

"How else would you explain what's happening to me?"

"Shit, I don't know. Why'd you even come here with me, then? Just to make me the laughing stock of the industry? Are you some kind of fucking career assassin or something?"

"No, of course not. I'm trying my best to remember things, man."

"This shit is hopeless. I quit," John threw his arms up and started walking down the hallway towards the elevator.

"Come on, John. Get back here, man. Please!" but he had already entered the elevator and taken it back down to the lobby. Alex looked into Howard's office. He was still on the phone. He entered anyways and sat down at his desk.

"Uh-huh. Yeah. No. Fuck no. Look, I gotta go—" and then he hung up the phone.

"Where's Johnny boy?" he asked.

"He's gone." Alex told him.

"Never liked the guy anyways. Now, did you get your mind straight about this pitch?"

Alex felt ashamed as he shook his head and said, "No, Howard. I really am sorry."

The contempt came back into Howard's eyes.

"Maybe you can coach me on what to say for this meeting, and maybe things will start coming back to me. I'll try to remember things. I really will, but I need your help and—"

"Just get out." He said firmly and emotionlessly.

"But—" Alex started.

"—I said get the fuck out of my office. You're off the project and you're out of an agent! What do you think about that? Jog any memories?"

"Sir, I assure you—"

Howard picked his phone back up. "Security. Get this nobody out of my office."

"That's not necessary. I'm leaving," Alex said and briskly walked out of the office, right past the security guards coming to get him.

He left the agency and realized that he did not have a car to get back home. Nor did he have any money. He started walking back towards West Hollywood, realizing that the meeting could not have gone any worse. And what's weird is that he actually took a slight comfort in that.

XXXI

Candace wondered whether or not it was a mistake to drive all the way down to LA just to see him again. She had laid it all on the line already, and since it was so soon after that, she worried that she might look pathetic now.

But he did sound genuinely happy at the idea of seeing her again when she called him up earlier. So she turned her radio up and slowly let her doubts melt away as she continued down the Golden State Freeway.

Alex cleaned his place up a little bit. It wasn't really that dirty to begin with, but he felt the need to make it a tad more presentable. After the oddly surreal defeat he had experienced in Howard's office earlier in the day, Candace's imminent arrival breathed new life into him. He packed fresh bud into the pipe and put the tequila back into the freezer so it would be cold by the time she got there. He opened the screen door, which was more or less his only real window, and let the 'fresh' air filter in.

He took a quick shower and put on a clean pair of clothes. He even brushed his teeth and made sure to wear deodorant. As tempting as it was to take a few shots of tequila to ease his nerves, he decided to stay completely sober for her.

A little over an hour later, the buzzer went off. Alex went over to the intercom and pressed the big black button.

"Candace?" he asked.

"Hey Curly, want to let me in?"

When he opened his apartment door, she stood there in a pair of faded jeans and a pink tank top. She dropped her bags and hugged him tightly.

"It's good to see you," she said in his embrace.

"Let me grab those bags for you," he said as he picked them off the ground and took them over to his bed. "There's a fresh pipe packed with some strain called Trainwreck. I got some tequila, too. I figured we could chill here for a bit and then go grab a bite to eat."

"Sounds great," she said. "Thanks for having me down."

"No problem. It's good to see you, too."

When they had both smoked and drank their fill, they walked to a hip new chili restaurant that Candace had read about and wanted to try. The waitress sat them at a high-rise table on the patio and they ordered a bottle of pinot noir.

"How have you felt since you've been down here?" she asked him.

"Okay, I guess. LA feels about as familiar to me as Guerneville did. There is this Gavin guy I hung out with the other day who seems like a good friend of mine. Other than that, John took me to see my agent and I totally made an ass out of myself. He fired me, and so did John."

"Well that kinda sucks," she said, holding onto his wrist sympathetically.

He shrugged.

"How about the coffee shop? They're cool with you taking off?"

"They think I'm at some funeral for my already dead uncle. He's been dead for like ten years," she laughed, and he did too.

The waitress brought them their food. They had both ordered a Cajun chili with a side of different breads for dipping. The dinner was pleasant, and they talked to each other in that small talk kind of way that they were both so good at talking to each other in.

After dinner, Candace confessed to not being much for LA's nightlife of clubs and expensive bars, so they went back to Alex's place.

They drank and smoked a little bit more, and then played some card game Candace liked to play while intoxicated. Afterwards they crawled into bed together. They had sex and then lied there in each other's arms for a while. Just before they were both about to fall asleep, Alex whispered into Candace's ear.

"I love you too."

She cuddled nearer to his body and they fell asleep together, smiling.

XXXII

Alex walked barefoot atop the canopy of the great Amazonian rainforest. The trees below his feet were so densely packed together, it might as well have been a paved road that he traversed.

Toucans cawed and horseflies buzzed around him. From the jungle below, the crescendo of crickets mixed with the orangutans swinging from the trees. It was hot and humid, and Alex was drenched in sweat.

A shimmering from the east caught his eye and froze him in place. He stared at it, but had to shield his eyes because the light was just too bright. As it flew away from him, he caught a glimpse of it indirectly. He chased after it sideways, and as he got closer to it, could see that it had silver butterfly wings. The light did not appear to be coming from it, but rather seemed to be reflecting off of it.

He reached a point that he could not get any closer to it. The butterfly kept him at arms-length, and he ran after it at this interval for miles. His legs suddenly became very heavy, and he started losing ground. So heavy, that it felt like there were rocks in his pockets.

Using one hand to shield his eyes from the blinding light, he reached the other hand into his left pocket, and found that it was filled with pebbles. He emptied them out, but was still weighed down. In his right pocket, there was only one rock, but it was quite heavy. It was about the size of his fist, but it was like trying to lift an anvil. While still running, he closed his eyes and used his other hand to help in getting the rock out.

To his touch it seemed like any old rock, but when he opened his eyes, he saw that there was actually a mirror embedded into it. With the rock-mirror in hand, and out of his pocket, he picked his speed back up instantaneously. He switched the heavy mirror into the other hand to keep the light blocked. In fact, it reflected the light away, and Alex was able to look at the creature a little more head-on. It was actually encrusted with diamonds.

With his new tool, it was not long before Alex was within inches of the butterfly. He leapt after it and caught it in his palm. He closed his fist over it, but the light still shone through. Before he knew it, the light was shining through the rest of his body, too.

Suddenly he disintegrated into smithereens and found himself swirling in outer space within the post-explosion of collided stars. He fused with the other star matter surrounding him at such a rapid rate that he liquefied.

He poured back down towards the rainforest canopy on earth. He rained down the trunks of the trees and through the branches and into the rainforest soil. He instantly soaked into the warm, moist earth.

When Alex opened his eyes, he found that he was lying on a red silk bed that was located within the center of a verdant bower. Flowers and vines and birds and fruit trees surrounded him, and a gentle stream flowed beside him. He was alone on the bed, but there was another pillow placed next to him. He rolled over onto the other pillow and noticed that there was a familiar scent upon it. Burying his head into it, he deeply inhaled the aroma and let it filter through his body. It did not take long for him to realize that in that scent, he had rediscovered Stella.

XXXIII

When Alex woke up from his dream, he saw Candace lying next to him, curled in a ball. Every nerve in his body went hot and cold at once. It made him nauseous. *What have I done?* He asked himself.

But how could it really, truly be his fault? It was by fate's hand that he ended up inside that redwood tree. Likewise, it was fate that Candace's dog found him there. It was not his fault that Candace was the one who found him at a point when he knew nothing about himself or about anything in the entire world.

Had he been who he always was, prior to his amnesia, he would have never forsaken Stella for anything. He would have rather cut his own tongue out of his mouth with broken glass, stabbed pencils into his eardrums, sewed his lips shut with yarn, and poured acid into his eyes.

And now that he had betrayed Stella, what course of action should he take? Should he reach over Candace's shoulder with a pillow and bring it up into her face until she couldn't breathe anymore? If he got rid of her, there would be no direct evidence of his infidelity. But Stella would be able to tell everything from his eyes the moment they first saw each other again. The betrayal and the cover-up. There was no hiding anything from her. And she was so pure of heart that him killing Candace, who was ultimately so very innocent of any wrongdoing, would make her even more upset than his stepping out on her.

Should he kill himself? That way it would keep him from directly harming either Stella or Candace. Sure it would break both of their hearts, but neither one of them would be mad at him. While he did not feel as strongly for Candace as he did for Stella, he knew that she loved him and did not really want to hurt her either.

Then he remembered that he told Candace that he loved her last night. Oh God.

Should he just explain to Candace that this was all a mistake, that he belonged to Stella for eternity, and had he remembered that he would have never gotten involved with Candace in the first place. Maybe if he let her down as gently as possible, she would not kill herself? Then he would just come clean with Stella and tell her exactly how it all happened.

But how could he even begin to find Stella? From where did he know her? Was it LA? That didn't seem right somehow. He didn't even know who his own family was or where they currently lived, except for the vague knowledge that his mother had passed away. Surely what remained of his family would be able to help him find Stella. And what about his friends? Gavin might know. So might John for that matter. When her scent came back to him, so did her image, but nothing that was tangible or could provide any clues as to her whereabouts, though. Nothing else about his previous life.

As he watched Candace sleeping, he continued to ponder what course of repentance would be the best one for him to take. As if she knew he was staring at her, she woke up and rubbed the cobwebs out of her eyes. She blinked a few times to adjust to the sunlight coming through the blinds, and then yawned.

"How long have you been watchin' me sleep, Curly?"

Alex forced a smile. "Just a little while."

"Awww…that's cute," she said and kissed his cheek.

Her lips were soft, but they made Alex feel dirty. He wanted to ask her if she knew anything about Stella, but realized how unlikely that would be. She sprung out of bed and put her pink bathrobe on.

"'Spose to be a nice day today," she said to Alex, who did not respond.

He was kind of blanked out at the time being. She just shrugged at the non-response and walked into the kitchen area. Even in the unlikely event that she knew of Stella, would Candace tell him anything about her? Or was she part of some greater conspiracy to keep Alex in the dark about everything?

Either way, Alex found it impossible to confront Candace. He'd have to look elsewhere.

He had done his best to engage with Candace in the small talk that she kept throwing his way. Every word she said killed him a little more inside with its meaninglessness. Everything that kept Alex away from Stella was meaningless. The first thing that Candace said all morning that legitimately caught Alex's attention was,

"So my friend Denise should be coming here any minute. Do you want to go check out the tar pits with us?"

"Huh, uh, no. I'm fine staying here and um, writing," he said.

She looked at him kind of funny.

"What the hell's up with you this morning, Curly?"

He could barely focus on her. "I don't know, maybe I'm just a little sick or something."

She put her hand up to his forehead, "You don't have a fever. And your color's good. You don't look sick."

Alex just stared off into space.

"No, you're not sick. It's something else," she said and shook her head.

Her phone rang and she answered it.

"Yeah girl, I'll be right down. Yeah, okay," and then she hung up. She walked right up into Alex's face. "You sure you're okay?" Alex nodded.

She shrugged. "I hope you feel better as the day goes on. I'd like you to eventually meet Denise. Doesn't have to be today, but I grew up with her, you know."

Alex gave her another blank nod. "Okay. Will do." He said. And then she left him there in the apartment.

The first thing he did was go over to the phone and call Gavin. There was no answer, but he left a message on the machine requesting a call back. Next he dialed John's cell phone number from the card that he still had in his pocket.

"What do you want?" John asked him, rather coldly.

"Do you know who Stella is?"

"Stella?" John repeated, "You call me up to ask about some broad? I thought you were calling to apologize or say you made things right."

"Look John, I'll make everything right if you just tell me what you know about Stella."

"You've really fuckin' lost it, man. And to think that you were once so goddamn talented. It's really a shame."

"Do you or do you not know Stella?" Alex was not in a playful mood.

"No, you psycho. I do not know Stella."

125

And with that, Alex hung up the phone. Next he tried calling Howard, but his secretary would not pass his call through. Alex wasn't too bothered by this, if John didn't know, Howard probably wouldn't either.

He paced back and forth and realized he was running out of options. He poured himself a shot of tequila and took it down. Then another. The phone rang. It was Gavin.

"What's the emergency, man?" Gavin asked.

"Do you know anyone from my life named Stella?"

"Stella, huh? Well, I don't know, maybe. The war made it hard for me to remember names sometimes."

"She would have been the love of my life," Alex told him.

"Damn bro, I'm not sure about that. I've never really known you to be with any one particular girl."

"Do you at least know my real last name?"

"Now that, I did know at a point. I can't recall right now. But if you came down here man, and we cracked a couple of brews, I might just be able to remember it."

"Okay, I'll be there as soon as I can." Alex said and ran out the door.

XXXIV

Alex took the harbor freeway down toward San Pedro once again. It was midday and the port was bustling. The gigantic industrial scope of it all once again impressed Alex, though it did not distract him from his goal at hand.

When he got to Gavin' place, he was outside sitting on his stoop that was too little to be called a porch, drinking a tall can.

"What up bro?" he asked and gave Alex the rock.

"Anything come back to you?"

Gavin shook his head, "Nah, not yet. But that's why I started drinking. I think when you told me your real last name we were both fucked up, right?"

"Maybe."

"So like, I remember from my undergrad psych class that if you learn something while you are fucked up, it is easier to remember what you learned if you're fucked up again."

"Sounds pretty logical to me," Alex admitted. "I mean, what I really want to know is where I can find Stella. Since nobody here seems to know her, maybe my family does, but—"

"—but you can't remember who they are, either, huh?"

Alex nodded.

"Right. I actually didn't even know that Alex was my first name, but since everybody calls me it, I guess it must be."

"Damn dude, you really did a number on yourself, didn't you?"

"Yup."

Gavin took a healthy swig from his can.

"I feel awful that I don't know who this Stella chick is, man. Just awful."

"It's okay."

Gavin reached for another beer from the cooler behind him and tossed one to Alex as well.

"Maybe drinking a bit will do us both some good memory wise."

Alex cracked it open and took a swig.

"It's worth a shot, I suppose."

A few hours later, Gavin and Alex were both totally wasted. Neither one of them had remembered anything of importance. The more intoxicated Alex became, the more he realized that he didn't have much of a plan. For the time being, he was at least numbing himself to the pain and anxiety he had been feeling since he woke up that morning. Gavin was entertaining him with X-rated tales from his war days, and it actually helped Alex take his mind off of things. That, and all of the marijuana they were smoking.

"...and there was this one time in Cambodia that I fucked the shit out of this chick, like literally, the shit came out and it wouldn't stop for like hours ..."

And so went the rest of the night until they both gradually passed out on separate couches in the living room.

In the middle of the night, Alex sprung awake violently in a cold sweat. Gavin was no longer on the other couch, and from the look of things it appeared he had found his way into the comfort of his own bed and shut the door behind him.

Alex's mouth was hot and dry, so he took a bit of water from the sink and then splashed some onto his face. He stepped outside. It was chilly out there. It was always chilly in Southern California at night. Especially by the ocean. And even more so since Alex had only a T-shirt and shorts on.

From Gavin's front yard, the lights of LA's port shone like a million souls against the pitch-black background of the nighttime sea, stuck mid-air on their way up to heaven. Alex walked toward the spirits, and before long, passed them by. He soon found himself in Point Fermin Park.

The lighthouse had not been operational for half of a century, but that night it shone out over the cliffs and into the water, lighting up a path from the harbor's shore to Catalina Island. Or maybe it was just the suggestion of light. Alex couldn't tell. He climbed over the stone fence at the park's edge and made sure to keep his footing as he walked towards the metal fence a hundred feet away and to the west. He crawled underneath, and made his way into Sunken City.

The fact that no light came off of the ocean made it hard to see around the place, but the ambient light trickling in from the port made it manageable. One false move, though, and that was the end of things. And Alex wasn't exactly moving with great caution.

He hastily climbed up and down the series of asphalt road fragments and rock inclines. He passed by the sounds of two teenagers having sex in the cover of darkness, and by the rattle and hiss of somebody tagging a rock with spray paint. He scaled the narrow ledge that hung over a rocky death below him that he could not presently see. He heard the waves beating against the craggily shore, though. Next he crossed the narrow footing that projected out over the cactus patch and heard coyotes howling at the moon. He walked past the patches of wild fennel, and then climbed down the jagged earthen edifice that led down toward the rocky shore.

It was high tide, and when the waves moved in again, they soaked his feet. He walked a little further until he reached the sea cave. He thought he heard a bear or some more coyotes in the cave, but he didn't even stop to blink. He soldiered right on into the darkest corner of the cave, and with the waves nipping at his heels, he pulled the tiny fishing boat out from its resting place and haphazardly set sail into LA's harbor.

XXXV

The water was rough, and Alex felt like the two oars that he had were not much use against the power of the liquid darkness below him. He just moved along where the waves decided to take him.

The further and further he got out into the ocean, the more familiar it all looked to him. At first he was not sure how to account for the familiarity. But then in a flash of lightning, another big chunk of his memory came back to him. He remembered the uniform blackness of his journey through space-time, and also his boat ride through the Chaos. He remembered the manipulation of the elements by the King, and how that particular boat led him to his mother. Was this boat leading him to Stella? If so, what eternal monarch must he do battle with this time around?

Then as if a spell fell upon him (or maybe it was the alcohol finally catching up to him), he suddenly passed out upon the boat's stern. When he woke up, it was high noon already. The sun had a reddish tint to it, and he was now so far out at sea that all he could see for miles in any direction was the choppy blue waters of the Pacific Ocean.

PART IV: THE ISLAND

XXXVI

There was no relief from the sun. Alex had no cover to place over the canoe, except for the T-shirt that he was wearing. He had blisters all over his face, neck, and hands from two continuous days out in the open with no sunscreen and not even a cloud in the sky.

He finally figured out that if he curled up into a ball as flat against the bottom of the boat as possible, and tied his shirt through the oar hooks on each side – he could create something that resembled a canopy. His T-shirt was not made with the highest thread count, though, so some sun inevitably bled through.

Under his canopy, he became deliriously thirsty. He had already been hungry, but since he had no food to satisfy that drive with, it was now being replaced by an unrelenting thirst. All of his sinuses were dried out, and the migraine that pounded at his head as a result was maddening. Furthermore, he didn't really have room to move around in underneath his makeshift canopy. His bones were starting to get sore from lying directly on the hard wooden floor without cushion. He felt like bits of his skeleton were chipping away inside of his skin.

His only comfort was the fragments of memory that he had involving Stella. Her smiling face and her scent. The purplish tint to her auburn hair when under direct sunlight. The feeling of holding her close to his own body. Her softness.

But this comfort came with the pain of realizing she was very much not there with him. If he called out to her, she would not answer. That even if he was back on dry land, he would not know how to find her.

If he slept, he may be able to find her in his dreams. But he could find no sleep upon the open water. At least no longer than thirty seconds at a time. It may have been slightly longer than that, but it was hard to judge time in any exact ways out there. He tried figuring out what time of day it was or how long had elapsed in any given interval by studying the sun and the moon's positions, but he got the feeling that they were not being totally honest with him. They would stay in the same place in the sky for hours at a time, and then at other times, move across it like pinballs trapped inside of a machine.

The Pacific had been choppy the whole time he had been on it. One would think that after a couple of days, Alex would habituate to the initial sea-sickness he had felt, but he did not. In fact, it grew exponentially worse with each passing moment. He had been hopelessly nauseous for more than 48 hours at this point. He was covered in his old vomit and reeked even to himself.

And though the sun was so harsh that his skin was peeling away from his body, the temperature even during the day was cold at best. At night, Alex was surprised that he did not freeze to death, or at a minimum, develop hypothermia. At least at night, his skin caught a bit of a break from the sun. Since his skin was damaged, though, it was quite itchy as the healing tried in vain to take hold. He tried not to itch it because when he did, his skin started to bleed immediately. But sometimes the itching was so overpowering that he could not help it.

He tried telling himself that it was not his fault for loving another woman, that fate thrust Candace before him at a point of great confusion. He was certain that the temptation would not have been acted upon if he had known about and remembered Stella. But he had not at the time. He had not known anything at that point.

But what ate at him the most was that part of him that wondered if he did know deep down. Subconsciously. How could one forget true love? How could one forget a blood oath? Maybe, just maybe, if he had waited long enough, he would have remembered everything about her, remembered enough to be able to find her again. The space amnesia might have worked itself out in due time. If he had just let it.

This fear, coupled with the sheer physical drain of his journey at sea, led him to a state of inactivity so grave that he did not eat or drink for days. He became famished. Weak beyond anything he had ever experienced. And he could not move, for he did not trust himself to move. And while he stayed immobile, he tried pushing the sin of Candace deep down inside of himself. So deep that he would never see it again. He focused only on Stella, as a hermit would fast and purge himself in a cave in the name of his god.

But alas, he knew nothing but the lonely motion of the waves and the caking of the salt in his hair and eyes and nose and ears and lips. He had not seen a single soul upon the sea, not even one of those great big freighters that come into LA to trade goods from all over the world. Dolphins, whales, and turtles passing by were his only companionship. So far he had not spotted any sharks, though he knew they lingered below him somewhere, waiting patiently for a taste of blood.

***

The day somehow made it into night again with Alex still living, but his skin was starting to sag off of his bones. A wave of darkness crashed into the boat and nearly capsized him, but he managed to stay upright. It filled the boat with water, though, and Alex had no way of getting any of it out. Even if he was given a bucket or something, he was so malnourished at this point that he wouldn't even be able to lift it. The water in the boat was freezing cold. He tried convincing himself that the burning of the salt in his gaping wounds was reinvigorating his body, but it hurt too badly for make-believe to take hold. His only wish was that he could drink some of the water. He was so very thirsty.

Actually, though, what was he waiting for? Water was water, right? Who cared if it had a little bit of salt in it? He could not afford to be so picky. He was going to die if he did not drink something. He would have drank his own urine, had he produced any to drink. But he did not. He stared at the salt water through dry eyes and rationalized that electrolytes in sports drinks were basically just salt added to sugar water, and athletes drank those after marathons.

He slowly craned his stiff, rubbery neck, and slurped up a bit of the seawater. It burned his mouth and took all of his energy in order to swallow it down.

As it worked its way through his weakened body, everything started spinning. Spinning, spinning, spinning so fast that it threw him into a fit of dry heaving. A curtain of red fell over his eyes, and then it started flashing. Spinning. Flashing. Red.

XXXVII

The spinning had violently stopped. The redness remained, though. He had not realized it, but his canoe had crashed into the rocky shores of an island.

He was laying face down on the hot white sand, and the only thing that he was truly conscious of was the smell of meat being cooked over an open flame. Alex fought through the red to try and get himself towards the meat, but he ultimately could not even budge a finger.

The smell of the meat was coming from a rotisserie that twenty or so members of the primitive native population were having on the beach. They were hairless creatures and mostly naked, covered sparingly with garments spun out of a rope-like material. Their most distinguishing feature was the fact that their skin was so bright white that they might as well have been covered head-to-toe in glossy white house paint. And the shininess of their skin was enhanced by the perpetual sunlight that reflected off of it.

Though Alex was unaware of them at the moment, the members of the tribe were hyper-aware of his sudden existence on their secluded island.

After a brief discussion amongst themselves in their native tongue (which consisted more of handclaps and a hissing type noise than words we'd be used to hearing) debating who or what Alex was, they had decided quite simply that he was either a god or a demon.

Some of the natives had voted to kill him and burn him along with the wreckage left over from his boat. Some of the natives thought that the shaman should be consulted before any action was taken whatsoever. Some of the natives thought that he was already dead, since he was not moving at all. A majority of those present at the roast, though, decided that if Alex was a god of any sort, treating him with anything but the utmost reverence would bring on the eruption of the volcano at the center of the island, Mt. Heliotrope.

Two of the male warriors cautiously approached him with their spears ready. When Alex did not respond to them moving closer, the one gently nudged him with the blunt side of his weapon to see if he was still living. He was, but barely. The other native kicked away a rat that was chewing at Alex's ribcage. He then knelt down and threw Alex over his right shoulder. They headed towards the jungle with him.

Then Mt. Heliotrope, which was clearly visible to them from their current vantage point on the beach, started to rumble. The natives gasped in terror and talked nervously to themselves. The man carrying Alex fell to his knees at the force of it, but somehow managed not to drop Alex. He picked himself back up onto his feet, and continued towards the jungle with Alex. The volcano quieted down for the rest of the night, but the natives did not.

XXXVIII

The natives had placed Alex in a verdant slice of the jungle about a half-mile from the coast. They propped him up against the base of a giant lemon tree, so he at least had ample shade. He was barely hanging on, though. He didn't even have the strength to keep himself leaned upright against the tree, and he fell face first onto the sandy ground.

He was hardly conscious at all, but somehow his left hand became aware of a fallen lemon within reach. He did not have the fine motor skills to grab a hold of it, so he kind of wormed his neck towards it as the last vestiges of life were leaving his body. The piece of fruit was rotten and moldy, and though Alex could not open his eyes to see it, the rancidness helped him know where to place his mouth. He plunged his crooked teeth into the decaying skin and bit down. The small amount of water he received from that effort was enough to keep him alive for now, but not enough sustenance to allow him to move from where he laid sprawled out in the sand. In between long periods of depraved and tortured sleep, Alex woke up just long enough to bite down on the lemon one more time.

The fact that the lemon had become so fetid that maggots were crawling and spawning inside of it did not faze Alex in the least. The maggots actually added to his pathetic strength. This cycle of sleep and slow hydration lasted a full day before he was finally able to budge even an inch from that spot.

When he was able to move again, it was only at a crawl. The first place he dragged himself, almost by instinct more than by any sense he possessed, was to another fallen lemon. This one was not rotten at all. In fact, it was in quite good shape. Any supermarket would be proud to display it in their store. And in an encouraging step, Alex was able to grab a hold of the fruit and place it in his mouth.

He bit into it like he was biting into an apple. It was bitterly sour, but due to his currently diminished faculties, Alex did not notice. Instead, when he was done with it, he went back to sleep for a spell.

XXXIX

When he woke up, he noticed that his body was covered with rats. They had been gnawing at his knees and knuckles and elbows – mostly at his joints. He weakly brushed them off. As they scurried away, his stomach growled in discontent. He went to get up, but realized that he could barely crawl.

He had managed to eat a few lemons at this point. He was sure that was the only reason he was still alive. Alex figured that it would take a while to die of malnutrition, though he had not had any fresh water for several days now. Then again, he supposed the juice in the lemons counted for something. He found himself craving eggs, toast, and coffee.

His nostrils were so arid that his nose constantly bled, and he could tell that his septum was covered in open sores. He had been keeping his eyes closed in an effort that he figured might conserve energy. When he opened them back up, the sun shot through them like a drill through his tear ducts. The veins in his eye sockets pounded to the point of bursting.

He tried getting up, but he simply did not have enough energy to pick himself up. So he just lied there, thinking of rats and lemons and Stella, hoping that he might die sooner than later.

He was barely cognizant of a rustling in the bushes in front of him. He wanted to see what was coming towards him, but he could not. The closer the footsteps got to him, the stronger the smell of meat became. Alex began to shoot saliva blanks out of his charred tongue. Then voices, but in a language that was not like anything he ever heard before. And then he passed out.

Two naked men came out of the bushes and sat next to him. The one was holding cooked meat on a stick. After an initial period of hesitancy, the man with the meat placed a piece of it in front of Alex's mouth. They waited for him to eat it, but Alex only lay there motionless.

Eventually Alex came to and pulled on every reserve of strength that he had to bite down on the sandy meat in front of him. It melted in his mouth and then everything went black again.

When he got back up, after having been out for who knows how long, the natives with their meat were still there. The small swallow of meat from before gave him enough strength to stand up on his atrophied legs and take a good look at the natives. They were so fucking white. Alex tried talking to them slowly, but they understood no English. They just pushed more meat upon him.

Alex was only too happy to accept the offering and chomped down on it. It did not take long for him to eat all that they had brought him. They were delighted that their gift to Alex was so well-received. He washed the meat down with some fluid that the natives carried around with them in a sack of skin fashioned out of some animal. Under normal circumstances, Alex would have spit the liquid out due to its strong copper taste, but for now he drank it up. He started feeling like a real human again.

The all-too-pleased natives left the liquid pouch with Alex and went back into the bushes. Alex wanted to follow, but his legs were too atrophied to perform the task. He called out to them to thank them and to beg that they would stay with him, but his pleading went unheeded.

He crawled to a low-hanging tree that provided ample shade and fell asleep like the snake does to digest his meal. It was the first real peaceful sleep he had gotten since before he set sail from San Pedro.

XL

Now that his body had digested the meat and processed it into energy, Alex had a somewhat substantial reserve of newfound strength with which to pick himself up with and walk around. He still had the sack of skin with the coppery tasting liquid in it, but decided that he would much rather drink fresh water. Though not entirely sure where to find it, he decided that the timing was now propitious for him to go and search for a source. If he was ever going to be able to leave this godforsaken place and find Stella again, he would have to keep his strength up. He would also have to locate those glowing white humanoids that came and gave him the meat.

He wondered how many natives existed in this strange new world. Were they all part of one tribe or were there several tribes? Did they live in cities or towns or municipalities? Did they have post offices, and churches, and so on and so forth? How was their society organized? Could they be trusted? Why were they so fucking white? It almost hurt to look at them. Alex was even forced to shield his eyes the first time they came to see him, that is how white they are.

Then he started thinking that he was not even sure what kind of a place this was. The natives were dressed in practically nothing but stereotypical island-tribe rope clothing, like islanders would dress in from a movie. So maybe he was on an island. He knew that he was on the ocean before he found himself in the sand. And there was a crash landing. He remembered the crash. And the madness in between. The boat and the sand. The fact that there was sand spoke to it being an island. But maybe not, actually. It could just as well be a desert. A desert next to the ocean, though? That was more or less what LA was. But the primitive nature of the place spoke mostly to it being an island.

When the thoughts took a momentary pause in his brain, Alex realized that he had already been walking for some time now. He had not yet encountered any water, though. He did catch a few glimpses of the giant volcano in the near distance through the densely packed jungle trees. Surely if he climbed up the volcano to a relatively high point (assuming that was possible), he could get a better feel for where he was, where water might be, and where people lived. But did he have enough strength to make it to the volcano? Sometimes mountains and volcanoes and shit look closer than they actually are, and he had not seen any food or fruit on the way other than the ubiquitous lemon trees. No nuts or any live animals other than the free-roaming rats. No birds in the sky. No insects, even. Just rats. He would perhaps have to catch a rat in the very near future to stay alive. That was obviously what the natives had given him the other day. He saw no other sources of meat as he tried to navigate through the semi-beaten paths the natives must have created to get through the vast labyrinth of tropical trees, ostensibly to hunt or gather water. He used the volcano as his guide. More than that, the volcano was a way to ground oneself in some kind of reality. Like a compass or something.

And then over the bend, he heard the very distinct sound of water trickling over rocks. Running water. Flowing through this foreign land. A water that would ensure a reasonable chance of survival. The only means by which he would ever see Stella again.

The trickling was getting closer. It sounded like a gentle stream to Alex. Like a creek, maybe. And when he got to the point that he could see it, he noticed a distinctly golden color to the water. He figured that was just the intense sunlight, though, combined with his weakened eyes playing tricks on him. His first impulse was to jump in the small rivulet. There was enough water for swimming at this part of the stream, and its flow was lazy enough that it would not pose Alex any danger of carrying him away downstream helplessly.

He got to the shallow banks of the creek and lied down on his stomach. He formed his hands into a scoop and drew some water out. He poured it on his head first to cool himself down from his hike. The coldness of the liquid sent a tingle down his spine as soon as it hit his scalp. And then it ran down his face. It smelled kind of weird, actually. Not rotten, no, that wasn't it. It was a strong smell. A familiar smell that Alex could not exactly identify.

He scooped up some more and this time held it in his hands to study it. He brought it closer to his nose. Nail polish remover, maybe? It was definitely golden. That was not just some illusion caused by the sunlight and intense heat.

Dare he taste it? Was it safe to drink? Would it be contaminated with microorganisms? The water was flowing rapidly enough that some instinct told him it would at least be safe to drink, assuming it was actually water. The liquid that he was studying had slipped through the crack of his hands, so he went down and scooped another cupful of it out. He brought it to his mouth but stopped short of pouring it in. He was kind of scared to drink it. Was all the water on this island this kind of water? Or was this just some special stream, or a tainted stream, maybe? If he were to keep walking towards the volcano, would he not stumble on some other stream or lake, perhaps? He was not yet thirsty enough to be in pain. He had found this stream and reassured himself that he could easily find it again if he had to in an emergency. And he still had the sack of animal skin with him. There was always that, at least. It was kind of disgusting, but it did the trick. With that, he decided to carry on towards the volcano.

It was getting hotter the closer that he got to the volcano. It was massive, and Alex was not sure if the proximity to it was what was making the temperature hotter, or if the sun was getting more intense as the day went on. There were foothills leading up to it that appeared reasonable enough to climb. And there were giant caves with gaping mouths at the volcano's base. Even though Alex was still about a mile away, he could still clearly make out the impressive array of cave entrances. There had to be hundreds, if not thousands of them.

The volcano seemed to be rumbling. Alex was not sure if that was a perfectly benign occurrence with a volcano, or a precursor to eruption. He took a certain calm in realizing that it was out of his control.

And then he heard more running water. At this point he was starting to feel borderline dehydrated. Perhaps this water would be more like the water he was used to drinking. For all he knew, though, it could be a different part of the same stream below.

He approached it in due time, and when he got to it, he saw that what he was hearing was actually a waterfall running down from one of the volcano's foothills. There must be a source of water in the volcano somewhere, maybe some basin created by adjoining foothills and rain water buildup. So far it had not rained the whole time he had been there, though. The closer he got to the waterfall, the more golden the falling water seemed to be. It could just be because he was still at a slight distance from it.

He wearily proceeded uphill for about a half of a mile. Before he could get any closer to the waterfall, his path uphill was abruptly cutoff at a point where he had to scale over a canyon in order to continue any further. The narrow cliff dropped off into a pit of hardened magma rock that was at least three hundred feet down and jagged. He had the option of turning around and trying to find a way around this obstacle, but he was running out of energy. He had to make it to higher ground as quickly as possible, as that was the only way he would be able to make the best guess as to which direction he should proceed for food, water, or to try and get more help from the natives.

He very precariously began to inch his way to the other side. The narrow ledge was about a hundred feet long. He was only able to side-step it, as there was not enough room for him to stand otherwise. Alex tried finding rocks in the cliffside that he could grab a hold of for support, but alas, there was nothing to cling to. He therefore moved very slowly. With every mini-step towards his goal, the ground below him weakened by a bit. Pieces of the rock ledge below him broke away as he progressed. He could hear the loosened rock tumbling down the side of the cliff down into the hardened lava pit below him. It was so far down that he could not hear the rocks hit the floor of it. He tried not thinking about the drop, but he still thought about it every second of his crossing. In the span of a few minutes, he had envisioned himself falling to his death or to serious injury at least a few hundred times. He was not sure it was worth it, but something inside of him told him that inaction would be even worse in this scenario.

Eventually, he made it across no worse for wear. A few hundred feet in front of him, there was a small lake that appeared to be fed by the waterfall in the distance. He approached it as quickly as possible and discovered upon closer examination that it too was tinted gold. So that's the way it's going to be here, huh? Alex was more than a little confused by it, but decided that the suspense was killing him even more than his growing thirst.

He approached one of the streams that emptied out into the lake, and at a point where the flow was fast enough to signify fresh, Alex placed his hands into a cup, and then brought the water to his mouth. When he swallowed it, he realized at once that it was tequila.

Needless to say, this did not excite him in any way whatsoever. He wanted water. He needed water. Tequila was his favorite liquor, but at this point, it was nothing short of a disappointment. His thirst was still there, and realizing that water might be harder to come by than he had anticipated, he opened up his animal skin and took in some of the bitter liquid. It was not good by any stretch of the imagination, but it sated him somewhat. He soldiered on uphill in the baking sun.

Though he had made it pretty high up into the foothills, he was still nowhere close to the rim of the volcano. He was, however, close enough to get a pretty decent lay of the land. He was able to determine that he was in fact on an island. It was a small island, maybe ten miles across and five miles wide. Most of it was jungle land. From his vantage point, he had a panoramic view of the entire island, yet somehow could not find any kind of dwelling place that the natives would be contained in. It was solid jungle. And as far as a source of water goes, he could tell straightaway that every bit of running water was golden in its flow.

The natives were human, though, how did they survive on only tequila? Maybe they adapted to it through evolution. Then he remembered the animal sack he had strung around his neck. Whatever the liquid inside of it was, that was how they beat thirst. But what was that? He opened it up and took another swig. Very coppery. A little thicker than water, but lesser than a milkshake. Maybe it was some kind of tree sap or something? What it reminded him mostly of was blood. That's gotta be what it was. Rat's blood. What the hell was he supposed to do, then? Survive entirely off of lemons and rats? There was no way that was possible. Furthermore, he would have to figure out a way to even hunt the rats. He had never even killed anything before. Sure, he had eaten his share of hamburgers and steaks and fish and so on, but he never personally hunted them and then ate them. He did not have the skill set.

And then a stroke of luck finally swung his way. To the right of a fallen tree that lied before him were two dead rats. They were freshly dead, too. No maggots had yet claimed their carcasses. He walked over to them. They both died with their eyes open, and their corpses were staring directly at him. How could he eat them while they were looking at him? How could he eat them raw? He decided that he wasn't that desperate. He still had some dignity, goddammit.

He picked up two dead twigs next to the base of a lemon tree and started rubbing them together like he had seen in the movies. That would cause a fire, right? Nope. No fire. He supposed that he needed kindling. He walked around and gathered up dead leaves and other fallen twigs. He set them in a pyramidal pile, and then proceeded to rub the sticks together just like before. There was some smoke, but no fire. He rubbed the sticks together so hard that he broke them both in half. He picked up two more and tried again, and again he failed. Two more, and again he failed. Two more and again he failed. Two more and again he failed.

He was now totally starving. The energy he had exerted climbing up this high was substantial in itself, but trying to start the fire all but wiped him out. He opened up the animal skin, and to his surprise there was none of the bitter liquid left. Shit, he thought. Now what? He crawled up to the trunk of a lemon tree and grabbed a fallen lemon. He took a bite from it like it was an apple. These lemons were outstanding, but they were starting to burn his stomach. All of the citric acid of the past few days had started to build up in the lining of his stomach. He could eat no more. He threw the half-eaten fruit down to the sandy ground, leaned against the trunk of a tree, and closed his eyes.

When he woke up, he was so hungry he could eat his own hand. And his thirst was just as close to killing him. Out of the corner of his eye, he saw the two dead rats still there, slightly more fetid. He had no choice, he had to eat one. Fire or not. He approached them and knelt down to look at them more closely. They were still staring at him through their dead eyes. They were daring him to place them in his mouth and swallow. He understood the taunt, and knew he had to respond to it. He had some trouble picking one of them up, though. His hand got close to the cadaver, but couldn't get himself to touch it. The bacteria that must be on the corpse grossed him out even still. He knew he was in bad shape, though, so he closed his eyes and reached down and grabbed a hold of one of them.

There was still some basic human instinct inside of him that could not eat it raw. He put the hairy dead thing as close to his mouth at his mind would allow him, but ultimately could not take the next step and bite down. He placed it back on the ground gently. He knew what he had to do.

Alex tepidly walked down to the tequila lake that was just below him. He bent his neck down and took sip after sip of the golden stuff. After he could take no more down, and felt that he was sufficiently drunk enough, he walked back up to the dead rats. Though he was still hesitant, he picked one up, and brought it towards his mouth. He decided that the meat by the ribs was probably the easiest to go after, so he closed his eyes and chomped down into the skin.

155

He felt the bristly hair upon his tongue first, and then the piercing of the muscle mass and the clang of his teeth against the rat's ribcage. Next came the flow of the cold congealed blood through his teeth and gums and down his throat. The taste confirmed that what he had been drinking out of the animal skin was in fact rat's blood. He tried to take another bite, but found that he could not. It did not matter how much tequila he had drank. He dropped the chomped-on rat and walked away as fast as he could.

The rancid chunk he bit out was still in his mouth and he finally willed himself to swallow it down. As soon as the sliminess hit his stomach, it mixed with the acidic buildup from all the lemons he had been eating. It created a nausea inside of him the likes of which he had never felt. He puked it all up.

After he vomited what little he had eaten, he continued vomiting. All he could taste was dead rat muscle, and all his teeth could feel was the marrow inside the bones of its decaying skeleton. Having nothing else inside of his stomach, his puking took the form of dry heaving. It eventually became so violent that he spewed out liver bile and what was left of the citric acid. As it rushed out of his mouth onto the sand, it foamed and reeked. The smell and sight of it made him want to puke his nothingness up even more, so he continued walking away from it as fast as he could. Eventually he walked far enough away to be out of the sight of the rats and the lemons and the tequila, and then once again, he passed out completely and thoroughly onto the jungle floor.

XLI

He did not have to see his own reflection in the tequila stream to notice his rapidly depleting body. After eating the meat that the natives brought him, he had gained a good deal of energy. Had he more successfully used that energy, he would have procured himself more to eat. Catch a rat, and at least try to eat one fresh.

All he had to eat, though, were the lemons and the corpses of the rats that he could not get himself to try again, no matter how much tequila he drank. And even though he was on the verge of starvation, he found himself getting sick of the lemons. He was positive now that the rats were the only animals on this island other than the maggots. And there were no trees other than those bearing lemons. And the only other vegetation that existed at all was the agave plant. It grew between the trees in the jungle and in great open fields that made up the valley beside the mountain range that the great Mt. Heliotrope resided in.

He found himself desirous of the rat's blood that the natives had given to him. That bitter, metallic sludge. Oh! What he would do for some of that. The lemon juice was burning his stomach. Or maybe it was the tequila. Or more likely, it was both of them.

Out of desperation he tried eating a leaf off of one of the branches of a lemon tree. The leaf was waxy and very obviously not digestible as soon as it touched his tongue. Sucking on the leaf produced a faintly numbing sensation in his mouth and teeth and tongue and cheeks. Like a localized anesthetic. He tried swallowing a little bit of the juices to calm his stomach, but it didn't really do anything.

He wondered, in a delirium brought on by his hunger and the heat, what Stella was doing at that very moment. Hopefully she was lazily gliding on some swing that faced the ocean. No, maybe not the ocean. The ocean was holding him prisoner. Maybe she could be jogging through a tree-lined, verdant park that circled around a small lake that had a view of her current city's skyline in the short distance. Maybe she was running past a couple of young lovers holding hands and laughing at each other's jokes. Maybe seeing such a sight broke her heart and connected her back into him. Did she know about him like he knew about her? Did she remember the eternal blood oath that they had sworn to one another? Did she even exist anywhere but in his own mind?

And then came a rustling in the bushes. And that same smell of approaching meat freshly cooked. The native man who held the meat last time was walking towards him through the bushes, but the man next to him was different this time. This man had a black robe on and walked with a wooden cane from which garlic and skulls dangled. He too, was native white, but he had a slightly less aboriginal quality to him. When he was close enough to Alex he said in near-perfect English,

"Hello stranger. We bring you more meat, and in an act of good faith, would like you to follow us to a feast we are having at the beach."

Alex's jaw practically hit the sandy floor.

"You speak English?"

"I hope I speak it well enough that you currently understand what I am trying to say to you," the black-robed native said, a bit self-conscious.

"Oh yes," Alex said. "I understand you perfectly well." He looked over at the man with the meat. "Does he speak English too?"

"No, he does not. I am the only member of the native population who can speak and understand English."

"I see. And yes, I would love to follow you to your feast. In fact, I would feel deeply honored to be your guest."

The English-speaking native bowed politely, "Delightful."

Alex was more than a little taken aback by this guy's command of the English language, a command that he felt might have exceeded his own.

"Sir, can I ask you how you learned to speak English?" Alex asked.

The shaman smiled and started walking back to the beach.

"I was taught English by my master who is now dead. He looked very much like you and he talked as you do, too."

They were now all strolling easily through the jungle. Alex was eating a piece of meat from the shish-kabob stick of meat that the other man was carrying.

"I am sorry that your master is dead. Was he from here, or did he land here like I did?"

"One day he was just here. Much like you are now."

"Would it be impolite to ask how he died?"

The native paused for a moment and then said, "No, it is not impolite." He pointed his finger towards the always-visible volcano and said, "He sacrificed himself by jumping into Mt. Heliotrope. Had he not, the volcano would have erupted and killed us all."

"How could you be absolutely certain of that?"

"The volcano god told him. My master was a sorcerer who spoke with the god of the volcano. And as a result of what I was taught as his apprentice, I am now what you might call the island's shaman, or high priest."

Alex was a little too weak to prod any further. He did not mean to pry at all, really. He was just kind of thrown off-guard by the shaman. Sure the shaman spoke English, but that in itself does not mean that the shaman and Alex would know how to talk to one another, or understand just exactly what one another meant by certain inflections of syllables or tone of voice. After all, sometimes best friends and lovers do not know what they are really trying to communicate to one another. That being said, they did have the common bond of being the only ones on a semi-deserted island who could speak to one another in English. Any bond with another human is a sympathetic one. And the language bond that Alex and the shaman shared made each one of them very curious about the other.

They were getting closer to the feast that was being held on the beach. The tribal rhythms could be heard pounding through the jungle air. Woodwinds worked their way through the forest like a creek that seeped into their ears. As the spell of the music took hold of all three of them, the shaman asked,

"How is it that you came to be on this island?"

"I traveled through space-time on a river. And that river led through the desert of Los Angeles, and spilled me onto the ocean. I got lost on the open seas and I got hungry. And thirsty. That is all I remember, other than bits and pieces of the crash that brought me here."

The shaman let the words sink in, and then said,

"A lot of people at this feast do not like you. But I told them that you are a good man. And the reason I know that is because you speak English. My master spoke English. And he was a very good man."

The meat-holder had walked the whole way with them too, but said not a word. Obviously, he and Alex would not be able to have a direct conversation, but they did happen to have a translator standing conveniently between them. Neither man, however, felt that they had anything to say to one another. Their respective pasts were just that wildly different that they could not relate at all. It was not that they adamantly refused to relate to one another, or anything like that, it was more that neither one of them cared enough to try.

"I wish I could have met this master of yours. Please excuse my saying this, though, I do not mean to be impolite or imprudent in any way, but I do not believe that any man is another man's master. Surely you see yourself as your own master, right? And only call him master as a sign of respect – not because you feel duty-bound to call him that?"

The shaman answered sincerely, "I call him master out of love and admiration."

And now they had gotten close enough where the scene became a little clearer to Alex. He was not sure what a native feast would look like, though he had some idea about such things from movies that he had seen. Drums being played. Meat being roasted on an open fire.

Naked people. Shouting and dancing and face paint. And flowers and blood markings and flute playing and the ocean at high tide coming up into the camp and licking at their toes. And it was exactly like that. Like completely how it would be in a movie. Exactly.

And it was not long before Alex was feasting on their meat and sharing the island's tequila and lemons with the natives. The meat was delicious. The music was pulsating. Alex completely lost himself in the joy of it all. He had not experienced such a pleasant out of body mystic excitation in his entire life. Alex was no drug addict, but he had experimented quite a bit. Nothing he ever took even sort of compared to the sense of euphoria that he was now feeling.

But alas, it only lasted for a few moments. Then he realized that he would probably never see Stella ever again. He was on an island that nobody knew existed. Nobody but the shaman's old master. But he was inside the volcano now. How was anybody ever going to find him? How would he ever be able to escape? He couldn't as of right now or for the foreseeable future make a boat. Or even a raft, for that matter. He might be stuck here for a while, or maybe even forever.

And then he looked over at the bonfire rotisserie. He could not believe he had not noticed it as soon as he got there. The carcass that was being cooked on the open flames was that of a human!

Was that the meat that he had been eating all along? Was it not rat's meat? Oh God! Alex hadn't seen any other animals on this island but rats and humans. That had to be a human cooking. He smelled so good. No!!! How could he think that?

The meat was good before you knew what it was, though, right? Was it or was it not? Alex couldn't admit it to himself, but then he realized that there was no point in lying to himself about it, either. He had eaten a human. So what, he was desperate. Any other human would have done the same thing in his situation.

He barfed once the gravity of the situation sunk in. He walked over to the shaman, covered in his own puke.

"Did I eat a human?" He grabbed ahold of the shaman. "Don't lie to me! Did I eat a human?"

The shaman looked at him sort of strange. "Of course you did, that is the meat that we've been feeding you."

Alex started barfing again, but he was so dehydrated from his last bout of vomiting that he was now only dry heaving. Violently dry heaving.

"What is wrong, master?" the shaman approached him with great care.

"Don't call me that," Alex slurred out between dry pukes.

"Why are you sick master? Do you not eat your honored dead in America?"

Alex could not respond.

"You had no problems eating it before, master."

"I am not your fucking master, man."

Alex was delirious and now stumbling from all the tequila he had drank. It finally caught up with him. The shaman produced a sack of animal skin from his cloak and handed it to Alex, but he smacked it away.

"That's human blood, isn't it?"

"Yes, master, it is blood. But it is rat's blood. We would never drink human blood. That would be sacrilegious."

The shaman picked up the sack and tried handing it to Alex again. Alex ignored the offering and made his way to the nearest lemon tree. He picked a ripe piece of fruit off of it and bit it through its skin. He chewed the leaves then, for a moment, in an effort to numb his mouth into forgetting what it had just tasted. He continued eating the lemon, and cried his eyes out. The shaman stayed close by him, truly concerned for his master's well-being.

XLII

Alex laid, sprawled out at the foot of a lemon tree. He was chewing on lemon leaves and rubbing them all over his body. Anything to try and take the feeling of just having eaten a human out of him. But it was not working.

He wanted to pick up a fallen branch and stick the jagged end into his arm. He wanted to cut into his skin and peel it away and then bury himself in the sand. There were no excuses for what he had done. Not the fact that he was starving to death, nor the fact that he had been tricked into doing it each time, either.

But then again, *does* the deception somehow absolve him in some small way? If they had never brought the meat to a starving man, he would never have had the chance to sin in such a way. So it was their fault. They took advantage of him. He was blinded by love and longing and a need to survive in order to find her once again.

So it was the natives who must atone for his sins. But which natives in particular? All of them? That seemed drastic. The shaman? Assuming he did possess some kind of magical capabilities, that would be far too much to overcome in his weakened state. And the native who came with the meat holder the first time around – he would not be able to identify him in a lineup.

But he had seen the meat holder twice now, and knew exactly what that man looked like. The meat had touched his hands directly before it was passed on to Alex's mouth. Perhaps he was the most culpable of them all. But wasn't the meat holder, in essence, just the messenger?

Maybe this was the rare instance in which the messenger must die.

What's worse? Alex thought to himself though his fragmented brain. Killing a human or eating one? Killing could at least be undertaken with some modicum of honor remaining intact. Or done in the name of something, at least. Cannibalism can make no such claims to higher ideals, or even attempt to. The veneration of the dead that the shaman alluded to was hogwash. Through no cultural lens could Alex see cannibalism as anything but the defilement of the dead. Certainly not veneration. With cannibalism, the dead's remains actually become waste matter as the body attempts to digest them. Where's the honor in that?

Alex found himself in the tequila stream closest to where he usually sleeps in the jungle. He was trying to scrape himself clean, but it did not seem to be working. There was, after all, no water for him to bathe in. Just the tequila. He had tried bathing in the ocean a few times since he had been on the island. It gets the body very clean, but there is no way to keep the salt from caking on your skin and making it itch afterwards.

And as far as personal hygiene goes, there was no such thing as a toothbrush on the island, either. Nothing he did seemed to get the human death taste out of his mouth. So once again, he used the tequila for that as well. As he bathed in it, from time to time he took a sip of the ghastly stuff.

He knew that as long as he had to stay on this island, he would inevitably run into the meat holder again. And every time that he would see the meat holder, he would be reminded of what he had done. He would be reminded of the taste of the flesh. He knew that he had to make the meat holder disappear if he ever wanted to straighten his mind out by the time he saw Stella again.

And the volcano rumbled along with his stomach.

***

The shaman was leading a prayer around the campfire. The feast was a veneration, as the shaman tried explaining to Alex before he stormed off into the jungle. Alex was an invited guest of the feast, so it was only right that he share in the feast.

Alex had thrown up the meat of the man who was being venerated, a most charitable, charismatic and wise man. A rejection of the gift that this man was so selflessly giving of himself to his native friends and to Alex, was seen by all on the island as a rejection of the veneration itself. The islanders were actually a very peaceful people, but such an act would normally warrant immediate execution of the one in violation of this sacred ritual. However, not only were the natives absolutely terrified of Alex, but it was well known amongst the natives that the shaman revered him.

As their high priest, the shaman called the shots on the island. Among a population as superstitious as the natives were, it was only natural for the spiritual leader to also assume the role of actual leader as well. They looked to him for guidance, wisdom, and as their conduit for the prayers and sacrifices that they offered up to the god of the volcano. Though the natives had certain base instincts of barbarism due to their primitive and isolated circumstances, the shaman saw to it that the population as a whole was benevolent.

The shaman had succeeded his master when he threw himself into the volcano to save the island. Since his master's sacrifice, Mt. Heliotrope had laid dormant. In fact, it had not so much as rumbled since then. But the moment that Alex crashed into the rocks upon the island's shores, Heliotrope once more bellowed out an angry roar.

And now that Alex had forsaken the veneration, the islanders looked to the shaman for guidance in how to deal with the sudden shock of it all. They were legitimately scared by Alex's arrival, and needed the reassurance of protection from the volcano god's wrath once again.

The shaman shouted spells into the fire and threw one of the dead man's teeth into the flames. The blaze shot up into beautifully colored fireworks. Not the patriotic kind that Americans love to display, but the spiritual kind that Americans have such trouble seeing.

Throughout the course of his prayer, the shaman managed to keep the islanders in his peaceful sway. He eased their hearts and minds, and gave no doubt that the veneration aspect of the feast had taken hold, and had not been sullied in any way by the vomiting. As he started on his final incantation around the fire pit, Alex re-emerged from the jungle unseen.

Alex felt like he was looking through eyes that were made out of the reflections of broken glass. He held a rock in his right hand and walked crookedly in a maddened state of drunkenness.

The shaman noticed Alex's maniacal approach, but did not miss a beat of his ceremony. He stayed focused on the prayer and ignored Alex completely. But some of the natives noticed Alex walking towards them. Those who noticed wanted to get up and run, but they dare not desert or interrupt their leader mid-prayer. To do so would add dishonor to dishonor and compound it. So they stayed seated. And the shaman kept praying. And Alex kept walking until he got to where the meat holder was sitting.

In a fluid motion, he smashed the meat holder's head in with the rock. He hit him without stopping until the meat holder was dead and bloody. The natives stood by horrified, but did or said nothing, as the shaman kept on praying, and the volcano kept on rumbling.

XLIII

Alex had dragged the meat holder's body deep into the jungle. Nobody on the island had tried to stop him. He had done it at first by some innate instinct to hide the body. He knew that he had done wrong, and he wanted to cover it up. He supposed that on some level he was afraid of the police. At some point as he carried him out, though, Alex realized that there was no real authority on the island to press charges or punish him for his crime. The shaman, maybe, but a servant rarely challenges his master, even if the servant is a leader in his own right. Maybe some natives would come out into the jungle and avenge the meat holder's death. But that seemed unlikely to him, too. He could sense their paralytic fear of him.

Once he realized that he didn't have to hide the body, he figured it would only be decent to bury the body. He had taken the meat holder's life, he did not wish for his soul to have to wander through limbo for all eternity.

Alex stopped carrying the meat holder's corpse at the first soft patch that he found in the root-choked sandy ground. The first spot in the earth that he'd be able to fit the body into as seamlessly as possible. If he was going to bury this man, he was going to do a respectable job of it. No pieces of him would be hanging out of the sand, or even protruding for that matter.

He began to dig into the earth with his hands. The sandy ground was giving way easily at first, but he quickly hit harder ground. At that point, he had only dug a hole big enough to fit the native's head. He had no interest in chopping the body up, so it would have to go into the ground whole. As he kept digging, though, it became quite clear that he had reached a layer of the ground that he would not be able to break through with his hands alone. Certainly not in his weakened state. But even if he had full strength and a shovel, he was not sure how much further he would be able to get down without some giant construction machine's help.

He was pretty sure that what he was coming up against was root. There were so many lemon trees in the jungle, and they all had such very shallow roots. He needed a tool. A rock might do, but he saw no rocks anywhere around him. He picked up a stick that lie a few feet away. He struck it into the ground where he had been digging, and it managed to make a few dents. Fresh scrapings that confirmed to Alex that he was digging through root. On the fourth shovel, the tip of his stick splintered up-twig, inserting several splinters into his skin. As the shards slid in, Alex winced with pain and then threw the stick to the side. He tried walking the pain off, but it did not help. The wood throbbed in his muscles. Pain went through each beat of his heart. He was forced to sit and rest against a tree.

The meat holder's corpse was ten feet away, and Alex could see that the rats were starting to show up. Alex tried picking the wood out of his skin, but it was no use. He needed tweezers or a needle in order to get it out. He was right by a tequila stream, and still had enough forethought to dip his hands into it to try and disinfect the wounds. It burned when the golden liquid hit his hands, but the burning took the throbbing away for a moment.

It occurred to him that if he drank some of it, the throbbing would recede to an even greater degree. But he was thirsty for actual liquid. He grabbed a lemon from a passing tree branch and bit into it. He had never tasted anything so sour. He almost threw it up, but avoided doing so by slurping up more tequila to try and neutralize his stomach.

His pain was getting worse. He was chewing on lemon leaves for all he was worth, and even squeezing the juices from them onto his wounds, but nothing was helping. And though it was so hot he had no real desire to eat, he could tell that he was violently hungry. He could feel the sinking feeling in his stomach and the sawdust taste of starvation in his mouth.

He did a quick scan for dead rats. He saw plenty of living ones hovering the meat holder's corpse, but no dead ones. Alex tried in vain to catch one. There were so many rats that it seemed almost a given that if he reached down he would pick one up, but the rats always managed to escape just in the knick of time.

The energy that he had exerted trying to catch a rat finally caught up to him. He collapsed onto the sandy floor. In his heart, he felt that this was the end of it all. He would never see Stella again. The number of breaths that he possessed was limited.

Then he looked over at the native's dead body. It was decaying rapidly. Maggots and rats were covering the corpse at this point. They crawled all over him and sunk their jaws into the feast Alex had laid out for them. The ritual of veneration had been inherited by the vermin, and they had accepted the task gladly.

And then a peculiar thought sprung into Alex's head. Why should he watch creatures as base and vile as rats and maggots feast as he starved to death? Was he too not entitled to the feast? In fact, by the meat holder's own cultural standards, the only way Alex could really honor his death and absolve the guilt was by venerating the corpse himself. With half as many breaths as before, he crawled over to the body on his hands and knees, more hands than knees, more pulling than crawling. As he got closer, he scared some of the vermin away, but some of the bolder beasts remained unfazed.

With his very last breath, Alex plunged his face into the meat holder. He could not open his mouth to chew, nor did he think he had the stomach for it. He was face down in the man's liver meat, and figured that this would be a terrible place to die. Defying his brain, his stomach reached up using some ghastly source of energy and sucked in like a vacuum that had just involuntarily been turned on. The fetid liver bile slid down his throat, along with some congealed blood. Alex felt his breath count increase instantly. He took another suck and found that he had slightly more energy. Soon, he was using his hands to claw away chunks of flesh and tendons and ligament and muscle from the cadaver. The splinters in his hand no longer bothered him at all. He was focused entirely on his animalistic urge to eat and keep eating until he was full, until he no longer knew what hunger felt like. He feasted with the base creatures, sharing the body and the blood with them. He liked the taste of it, and he liked that it was raw. He even liked that he could taste the rats' saliva on certain pieces of the meat.

Once he had his fill, he backed away. He took a few sips of tequila to cleanse his pallet. Not because he was disgusted, but for the same reason one would cleanse their pallet after eating a strong, aromatic cheese. Not that there was even that bad of an aftertaste, per se, but it was definitely a little too funky and alien to his taste buds to let it sit in the gaps between his teeth for too long unchecked.

He fell asleep under a lemon tree and dreamt of holding hands with Stella along the Cuyahoga River towpath. He reached his longer than average nose over and smelled her hair where her neck met her jaw and ear. He breathed her in over and over again, and she smiled as the water flowed gently beside them through the ample woodlands.

XLIV

On a certain level, Alex felt very badly about killing and eating the meat holder. But since killing him, he had figured out how to start a fire of his own. He cooked those parts of the corpse that had not yet gone foul, and then dragged the body off to the ocean.

It was night by the time he was able to move the body to the rocks by the shore. He propped the corpse up on the rocks, and figured that by the time high tide rolled in, the sea would take care of the rest.

The morning after, Alex woke up and checked alongside the rocks. There was no sign of the body anywhere. The waves had done their work, and now that there was no direct proof that he had ever killed the meat holder, all the islanders had to cling onto was speculation. He would not answer to the accusations of the islanders, certainly not without any direct evidence of his crimes. He would not recognize the islanders at all from this point forward. Especially not that ridiculous shaman. Who did he think that he was, acting all spiritual like that?

And who, anyway, could these islanders even appeal to in order to punish him for his vile acts? Their only option was to come at him directly, and there was no way that they would strike out at their master. They wouldn't even know how.

And since he had already stepped over the line once, he reckoned that it would be easier to do it again a second time. The killing would be slightly harder than the eating. Alex had already eaten enough lemons for a lifetime at this point, and knew that he did not have the skill to catch a rat. Humans were a lot easier to catch.

But these savages were clearly less than human. Sub-human. Cro-magnon, even. More similar to eating a monkey than it was to eating an actual man. It was the killing that he might not be able to do again so easily. Luckily, though, the tequila was ever-flowing, and he was sure that he could find courage enough in that to kill. Not much pride, though, perhaps. But who needs pride anymore? Pride of what? Pride of self? Ha! Alex was not even sure anymore who his self even was. A killer? A cannibal? A writer? The only thing he knew with any degree of certainty was that he loved Stella, and Stella loved him. And that he had to find her. If that meant killing and eating everyone on this island, even raw if he had to, he would do it if it brought him closer to seeing her again. The longer that he survived, the better those chances would be.

He rationalized that his survival was more for her sake than it was for his own. She needed him. He knew that she needed him. He would not deprive her of himself just so some savages could survive. To what purpose should they survive? They contributed nothing to the greater good of the world. It would be selfish of him, even, not to survive.

No one even knew that the natives were here. Only Alex and the old master had ever known. And if the shaman's own logic was followed (which it was by the entire native population), then Alex was the old master.

That afternoon, Alex went on the hunt. He still did not know where any of the natives lived exactly, but he had a general idea, so he went out towards that area with a sharpened spear.

As he walked around, he realized that the island that he was on was really quite beautiful. If one were able to pretend that the tequila was actually water, then the lush array of riverbeds and waterfalls and low drooping lemon trees would actually be quite serene.

He could not find a single native anywhere. He still had a little bit of meat on his person and decided to eat what he had left.

***

He had been focusing his hunt on the coast for the past few hours to no avail. No sign of the natives anywhere, and the sun was starting to get to him. He needed the shade of the trees. He was using up far too much energy. A nice full belly is enough to make anyone cocky, but once the tank is empty, the engine cannot run for long on fumes alone. He needed a real meal. Even a dead and decaying rat would do at this point. Anything other than another lemon, but that was all he could find in the densely thicketed jungle. His throat and his mouth were too dry and sensitive at that point, the acid from the lemon would eat right into his flesh. What little sustenance he could obtain from the fruit hardly seemed worth it. Ultimately, though, he ended up with no other choice. His basic animal instinct to survive prevailed, and he gagged a lemon down. He sat down at the base of a heavily branched trunk and allowed himself to rest and absorb the energy.

When he opened his eyes again, the shaman was standing there in his black habit, bowing before him. He raised his head upright and started walking away.

Alex got up to follow him, but the shaman had already created a sizable distance between them. The chase went on for a few minutes, without Alex being able to make up enough ground to catch the shaman. And then, the shaman disappeared into thin air. Alex stopped, and stared confusedly. He was drawn out of his momentary trance by the snapping of a branch underfoot by someone in the distance. He headed towards the noise.

When he caught up to it, he saw a native man who was only partially clothed, walking alongside a stream. He froze when he realized that Alex was coming from behind him. He did not run, but he turned his head around and looked at Alex with pleading eyes. Alex registered the eyes, but only thought that the pleading made them look that much more delicious. He took his spear and thrust it into the native's heart. His heart geysered blood out of his chest like a grape getting squashed out of its skin.

Alex made a fire and cooked him up. After he ate his fill, he decided to try and preserve some of his hunt. It would be easier to fire up some more meat at hand than it would be to find and kill another native. He remembered learning in school that salt was used as a very early preservation method. Even though there were tons of lemons, and plenty of tequila, sadly there was no salt on this island. Sand, but no salt. Unless somehow he could collect it from the sea? Could he even collect enough that way? How would he get the body to the salt? Smoking meat went back to the middle ages, maybe that could work. He did know how to make a fire at this point. He had no house with which he could smoke the body, though. He certainly was not capable of building one. The tequila might preserve the meat, but then again, it could just as easily decompose the meat for all he knew. Either way, it did not much matter. He quickly realized that he was a predator now. Predators do not have the option to preserve. The predator lives and dies by the hunt alone. He would just have to get better at finding his prey.

XLV

Alex sat atop the branches of an elegant lemon tree, scoping the jungle out. For a while all that crossed his line of vision were groupings of rats scurrying about. It was up here that he was reminded that the island had no birds to speak of. He was keenly aware of the rats being the only animal on the ground, but he had forgotten about the life that was supposed to be in the trees.

After a while, a plump female native walked alone underneath his tree. She's probably got a lot of fresh water inside of her, Alex thought, and her muscle probably goes down easily with all of the fat that is clearly surrounding it. He let her pass by a bit and then snaked down the medium-sized trunk using his jagged toenails to dig into the bark for extra support. When he reached the jungle floor, he was careful not to rustle any leaves or snap any twigs as he followed her. She did not seem to know that he was following her, and if she did, then she was too terrified to turn around and acknowledge him. Not playing dead, but playing dumb, maybe.

He kept about fifty yards between them for some time. She was taking him on a very twirly course through an unbeaten path, so he had to be extra sure about not making any noise. Her backside was beautiful. She was not wearing a top, and her back arched in such a way that he wished he could lick it.

It was hot, excruciatingly hot, and the wind was blowing heavily. It carried her native scent into his nostrils, and he realized that he was far past the point that body odor bothered him, in fact, he rather enjoyed it. He gradually gained ground on her, and had to admit that this game of cat and mouse was actually arousing him.

She crossed over a stream twenty or so yards in front of him. She made a good deal of noise sloshing through the shallow running tequila, causing him to wonder how he would continue following her unnoticed.

When he got to the stream and looked for any stones in the creek bed that might aid in his silent crossing of it, he only found two small rocks. He would have to go in as he was. When he went down the steep banks, he slid a little, and splashed as he entered the tequila. She stopped dead in her tracks and listened.

Oh, shit, Alex almost said out loud as he went face down, flat into the water. It cooled his body. She finally looked back, but he was too low for her to see him from where she was standing. She intently carried on her way, at a slightly more brisk pace. He grabbed one of the stones that was lying in the creek bed next to his face and rose up out of the shallow stream. She was on dry land, and had gained some ground on him. And now she was running. Alex picked up his pace a bit, but remained as stealth as possible. She entered one of the thousands of caves at the base of Mt. Heliotrope.

When Alex walked into one of the sandstone cave entrances, it was a lot deeper than he originally thought it would be. She was no longer at its entrance, but had now been swallowed up into the very bowels of the cave. It was dark in there, pitch black, and all he could hear was silence. Though he had no torch to proceed with, he went ahead anyways.

There was a musty smell in the cave. It was cold, too. Since he could not see, he ran nose first into a stalactite, and could now taste blood in the back of his throat as a result.

He had completely lost track of his prey and was entirely lost. He was alone with the absolute silence of the cave. The hunger was getting to him, too. Maybe this is where he will die. The blood from his nose would not stop running, and he felt millions of hairy legs crawling over his skin. Spiders, maybe? Who knows? Whatever it was, they were biting him over and over again.

He grew angry at that plump native woman for luring him into this godforsaken place. He was still holding the rock in his right hand and wanted nothing more than to crack her skull open with it. He could not wait to eat her brains raw and munch on her eyeballs in the darkness. He wanted her to be alive when he started feeding on her. He wanted to hear her pain. And then, all of a sudden, he heard a creaking noise in the distance.

And just like that, he started falling through the rock below him. Whether it was an earthquake or the cave collapsing in on itself – he kept on falling. And he was getting cut up something fierce along the way down.

When he finally landed on solid ground, he was in so much pain that he could barely see straight. He was able, though, to make out a dim light coming from up ahead. In agony, he dragged himself toward it. One inch at a time. He was sure that both of his legs were broken. Both of them. Still he pulled himself towards the light. An exit out of the tunnel, maybe?

But when he managed to pull himself closer, he saw that it was not sunshine there in front of him, but the light cast from a torch instead. There in a hollowed-out recess of the cave, was the plump woman he had been chasing, kneeling before a naked pregnant native who was giving birth. She was pushing and breathing as hard as she could. He pulled himself closer using his hands, grabbing onto the jagged sides of the rocky cave for leverage. How the woman was screaming! Alex got close enough to almost touch the birthing woman, but neither her nor the plump woman paid him any attention. They were completely dedicated to the task at hand.

"Why are you giving birth down here?" Alex asked, but there was no response from either of them. Just the screams of childbirth. He moved in a little closer, just as the head of the child started crowning out of her womb. He could not help himself from staring in amazement.

Pretty soon, the whole child was out. It was a girl. And the witnessing of her birth brought Alex to tears. He remembered his mother, and started to remember the kind of man she had raised him to be. He had forsaken her by the way he was acting on this island. He had forsaken her, and he had forsaken Stella. Alex realized then that it was up to him to seek atonement for his own sins. Nothing had been the natives' fault.

He got up effortlessly and realized that none of the bones in his body were actually broken, just bruised. He walked over and kissed the baby on her head. The mother and the plump midwife he had almost killed and eaten – he kissed them too, and then they kissed him.

Alex knew then what he had to do.

Brian Dyko

XLVI

The shaman's hut was in the shape of a cone. It looked sort of like a big tropical wigwam. It was constructed of clay and used lemon-tree bark for its roof. It had an open-air doorway and two slits in the side for windows. It was brownish in color, but the sunrise gave it a crimson hue. Alex walked through the doorway without signaling his entrance.

The shaman was not there. A black marble slab sat in the middle of the conical room. There was a cauldron close by the slab, and there was an altar closer to the wall. A creaky wooden rack of jars filled with herbs and potions and salts and urine stood along the wall at a right angle to the altar.

Alex noticed that in a darkened section of the hut was an iron cage with a small dog inside of it. It was wagging its tail. Alex went to pet it and then realized that it was really just a big fat rat. It gnashed its teeth and scratched at him through the cage.

Alex walked towards the slab at the center of the room. He noticed that there was an open book on top of it. The book was outlined by some kind of a golden dust.

"It is open to the same prayer that you left it open to the day you jumped into Heliotropa," the shaman said as he approached Alex from behind.

"Have you been behind me the whole time?"

"No," he replied, "I was downstairs and heard somebody walking around, so I came upstairs."

Alex looked around the inside of the hut and could find nothing that led to a downstairs corridor.

184

"You don't have a downstairs, I see nothing that leads down there."

"Just because you cannot see it, does not mean that it does not exist, master."

The shaman's insistence on calling him master was starting to get on his nerves a bit, but he was not there to pick a fight.

"I have come to you, shaman, to ask for forgiveness and redemption."

"Forgiveness and redemption for what?"

"Forgiveness for my sins."

"That is far too vague, master. Perhaps my English is not as good as yours, but can you please be more specific?"

"For the killing and eating of two natives, and for the intent to kill a third."

"The intent?"

"I did not end up killing her."

"This moment has been prophesied," the shaman bowed to him and disappeared.

His abrupt departure annoyed Alex. Having nothing better to do, he walked around the perimeter of the room. There was a painting of a volcano with two eyes on it in one of the darkened sections of the room. The one eye was open and yellow and on fire. The other was shut. There was a cave painted into the base of the volcano that looked very much like a mouth. And underneath the volcano's base was a pair of hands that was holding it up like a foundation. Alex wondered from where the shaman got the canvas and the paint.

The shaman re-emerged from the darkness holding a naked native man on a chain-metal leash. A collar was strapped around his neck and connected by more chains to a pair of handcuffs, and then from there, more chains attached to a matching set of anklets that were each chained to a very large coastal rock.

"You are wondering where I got the paint and the canvas from, and maybe even if I painted it myself?"

"I was wondering that, yes, but now I'm a little more curious about the naked man that you have chained up behind you."

"This man is a very bad man, master. He has broken many of your laws."

"Those laws are not my laws, shaman. They are yours."

"As you wish. Then let us compromise and agree to call them basic human laws."

"Have I not broken some of these basic human laws myself?"

"Yes, but you are a good man. Your soul can still be saved. His cannot."

"And how is my soul to be saved?"

"First you must trust me and trust the process. I have prepared for this ever since you leaped into the volcano. If you want it done right, you must submit completely to my judgment and care."

Alex paused to stare at the prisoner.

"Do not worry," the shaman said, "we shall not have to kill this prisoner in order to save you."

Alex figured that he had no choice.

"I give myself up to you."

"Your sins will soon be forgiven, master."

"Can you bring me back to Stella? Would you know how to do magic like that, shaman?"

"I deal only in the spiritual realm, master. I cannot manipulate physical reality to the extent that it would be necessary to do so in order to reunite you with your lover."

"Yeah, I figured as much."

"I hope you understand that I feel terrible for the limitations that I have in my magical capabilities, but please rest assured that I will do all that I can for you on the spiritual realm."

"I will gladly take whatever connection to Stella you are able to find me. And I will do so with no questions asked. Do unto me what you will, shaman. I want to be purified."

The shaman nodded gratefully, then proceeded to blow a fistful of the golden dust into Alex's face. As soon as Alex inhaled the first molecule of it, he was rendered unconscious. The shaman caught him before his head hit the floor, and proceeded to lay him down with the greatest of care. He walked over to the black marble slab and picked the book off of it. He read the prayer that it had been opened to since his master jumped into Heliotrope. He had never read it in full before that very moment. Then he placed his right hand on Alex's head, mumbled something into his ear, and then left the hut promptly thereafter.

XLVII

Alex was lying on the marble slab in the middle of the darkened room. The shaman had some wild herbs burning in the cauldron to the side of him. The marble was cold against the back of his body, as he was completely naked.

His arms and legs were tied to posts at each corner of the slab. The shaman had fastened him using rope woven out of the agave, and it was of a fiber thready and sharp enough to cut into Alex's skin if he tried moving. His neck was clamped down with an iron ring and his eyes were kept wide open. He was only able to see the black ceiling above him.

He could hear the bound and gagged prisoner to the left of him. The prisoner was being kept in the cage with the rat, and had not been let out for days. Their feces and urine were mingled into giant piles next to the bowls of water and gruel that served as their only sustenance. They had both eaten pieces out of each other at this point, as well. The shaman kept Alex awake through it all with an elixir that he said was part of the cleansing process. It tasted like the inside of a neon bar sign.

Although Alex had not been let out of the room either, he was at least permitted to roam freely within it up until this very moment. The prisoner spent the entire time confined to the rat cage.

All and all, Alex had found his time there to be rather peaceful. No matter the time of day, the room was always dark. There were things that could be seen in the dark, connections that could be made, that were entirely impossible to reach in the light of day alone. He had been completely able to recall his entire journey from the tunnel underneath the university art building, through space time, up until his present situation.

He was not able to find Stella in any of this, but the shaman assured him that he would not be able to right at the outset. Only a pure soul could tap back into a pure love, he said.

At first the prisoner howled in pain through his gags – day in and day out. He was now at the point of acceptance, and remained quiet for the most part. He would talk to himself from time to time, like people forced into craziness are wont to do, and he was currently doing that right now. Sometimes he and the rat would have growl fights, and sometimes scratch at one another's skin with teeth and claws. Alex was sure that they spoke a language to one another that was neither rat nor human, but rather a creation that naturally evolved by virtue of the situation that they found each other in.

Alex heard the rattle of the skulls and bones that the shaman kept on his walking staff coming at them through the darkness. And when he got to Alex, he looked straight into his eyes and said,

"Now I will find the evil that is inside of you."

He started rubbing his hands all over Alex's naked body. Starting with the neck first, he gradually worked his way down to the abdomen. He circled it with both hands generously and then picked his hands up and placed them right before Alex's kneecaps. He performed reiki on his kneecaps, and Alex felt strangely titillated by it. Then the shaman started rubbing his feet. He went into the satchel that he had been wearing around his waist, and proceeded to rub something rough like mulch upon Alex's feet. In a very low voice, he projected towards the ceiling and said something in his native tongue. He paused for a moment, and then grabbed a sharpened piece of bark and stabbed it right into Alex's gall bladder.

Alex was screaming, and so was the prisoner, as if it were contagious. The shaman pressed down on the wound to increase the blood flow, and then went over to unlock the prisoner from his cage. He ungagged him and shoved the prisoner face down into Alex's wound, and ordered him to "suck" in the native tongue. Alex could not see, but he felt the pressure of the prisoner drinking from his midsection. He could feel his teeth bite down and his tongue enter the hole that the shaman made inside of him. Licking it up, slurping it up, drinking with the thirst of a wild animal. It stung, and Alex screamed out some more. He howled from the depths of his being, but the shaman let the prisoner continue to feed.

Alex tried escaping, but when he struggled the ropes only cut deeper into his skin. The ropes were wet with his blood now. He tried escaping into his own mind, but all he could see was darkness. Darkness on fire. And then Candace leapt into his mind's eye totally naked. She was riding him and he could not get her to stop. He tried to shout at her to get her off, but as in any nightmare, he could not get his voice to work.

And just like that, she was gone, but the prisoner was not. He kept feeding on Alex for an indeterminate amount of time. Finally, the shaman pulled him off.

The shaman said a couple of spells into the bleeding wound and then shoved a salve from a root of some plant into Alex's laceration. The pain was gone. He untied Alex and then shoved some salve into his mouth.

"Swallow! Swallow! Swallow!" he ordered, and Alex did what he said. The pain and the wetness of the blood disappeared. The shaman cracked the metal ring off of Alex's neck with his staff.

"Rise!" He commanded.

Alex got up and looked down at his midsection. No bruises whatsoever. Same with his arms and legs. The prisoner was back in his cage, starry-eyed, and face covered in blood. The rat was licking it off of his face.

"You are now free of all your sins, master. The trial shall commence at daybreak."

"What do you mean, trial?"

"You are forgiven, but the sins themselves are not."

Brian Dyko

XLVIII

The courtroom was set up inside the shaman's hut. The black marble slab at the center served as the judge's bench. The prisoner was seated in the witness stand next to it, and Alex was at a table that was situated across from the bench. All of the natives were present in the audience.

The shaman walked out of the darkness, holding the skeletal remains of a human hand. He stopped at the black marble slab, upon which an empty stone box had been placed. With the skeletal hand held high above his head, using a spell, he simultaneously said in English and the native tongue,

"Before our master threw himself into the bowels of Mt. Heliotrope, I could not help but to try and stop him. Once he said a proper goodbye to me on the edge of the volcano's rim, he stepped off from it, and into the volcano's core. I instinctually thrust my arms out to save him, and was able to grab a hold of his hand before he fell out of my reach. I held onto him as his legs dangled into the fiery abyss. The magma from the volcano sent tongues of flame shooting upwards to try and claim him from my grasp, but my grip was strong. It was no matter to me that the heat was so great that I still have scars from the burns that those flames caused me."

The shaman uncharacteristically rolled up the sleeves of his cloak to expose his scarred-up arms. The natives in attendance gasped at the sight, and Alex too, was taken aback.

"And then out of the thin garment of clothing that was our master's funeral shroud, he produced a knife of very respectable size. Without saying a word, he swung the blade down on his wrist and severed his body from his hand. He fell down into the fires, and left me there holding the hand.

"With a heavy heart, I took it back to the hut to show it the proper veneration that it deserved. The skin and muscle that did not come off during the sacrifice, I washed off in the waves of the sea. And then to preserve it, I soaked it in the tequila stream behind the hut for a fortnight."

He then placed the hand inside of the stone box and placed the lid over it, chanting the whole while.

The shaman signaled for Alex to kneel before the judge's bench. He slid the stone box to the edge of the marble altar. There was a slit in the top of the lid, and a slit at the base of the box. The shaman poured a vase full of tequila through the slit at the top.

As the tequila passed through the stone reliquary, the hand inside of it closed its bony grasp into a fist, and squeezed the golden alcohol out of the liquid. By the time the tequila flowed out of the box and onto Alex's head, it had become water.

Alex at first did not expect this, thinking it would still be tequila. But when his sense of smell caught up with his mind, he realized that there was no aroma to the liquid that washed over him. He opened his mouth and let the water hit his tongue. It sent a jolt of calm through his entire body.

As he basked in the life-giving liquid, his past came back to him in its entirety. He had already re-found Stella in his dreams, and now in his madness, he was sure where to find her. He was sure of everything. Ohio. Central

Ohio. Columbus, specifically. She would be there, waiting for him. If only he could find his way back there...

The shaman walked over to the witness stand and stabbed the prisoner below the rib cage. He howled out in agony.

"Stay where you are at, master."

He said as he collected the dying prisoner's blood into a jar. Not one of the natives in the audience moved a muscle.

"Put your salve on him, what are you doing?" Alex demanded.

"The sins must first be put on trial."

He walked behind the judge's bench with the jar and held it over the stone reliquary.

"You said he did not have to die!"

But the shaman ignored Alex's pleading, and spoke spells into the prisoner's blood. He then poured it into the top slit of the sacred box.

"Do not move!" he commanded Alex.

This time in the reliquary, though, the master's hand did not clench into a fist. The blood simply ran over his hand and then onto Alex's face.

"Swallow!" the shaman shouted.

Alex reluctantly opened his mouth and let it flow down his throat. The shaman went over to the prisoner and placed his healing salve into the wound. When Alex took his fill of the blood, he moved away from the altar.

"What did this prove, shaman?"

"Take a seat, master, we wait for the verdict."

The prisoner was allowed to return to the natives, and he sat amongst them in the audience. Alex sat at the table at the front of the makeshift courtroom, facing the shaman, who sat silently on top of the marble altar.

At the center of the island, Mt. Heliotrope erupted violently into the sky, spewing its lava everywhere. Back at the shaman's hut, everyone there, including Alex, knew what had just happened.

"We have a verdict!" the shaman announced.

Something fell down onto Alex's head and split into his skull. The natives all died like they did in Pompeii, frozen in the present. And then the meat holder's body washed back onto the shore.

PART V: CLEVELAND

XLIX

"Stamp it and slide it, 10-06! Move it down the line!" a gruff voice commanded him from above. And then an elbow gently prodded his side.

Next thing Alex knew, he was standing on a car assembly line inside of a giant factory warehouse. It stretched out for miles in a malaise of enormous metal machines. The elbow belonged to a tall, genial man next to him who was wearing a backwards baseball cap, and had the name "Teddy" sewn onto a patch on his shirt.

"What gives, A?" Teddy said, half laughing.

Alex realized that he was at a large steel contraption that hung from a support beam above, and that his hands were gripping bicycle handlebars that were connected to the device by a pulley.

"We gotta goddamn quota to meet, 10-06! Stamp it and slide it down the line!" The hairy foreman screamed, as he hastily started down from his overseer perch with a clipboard and a cigar in his mouth.

"Pull it down man, Krumholz is gonna kill you," Teddy said between his teeth with urgency.

Alex pulled the handlebars towards him and the contraption slammed down on a malleable plate of aluminum, forming it into the hood of a car, before the conveyor moved it forward. Teddy slid the next piece of metal below his hands, and Alex repeated the motion.

The foreman grunted but said nothing, and turned around and went back up to his perch. This monotony continued for about an hour, though it seemed much longer, and then the whistle blew.

"Alright ladies, see you next week."

Everyone abandoned their stations and headed for the clock to punch out. Krumholz shouted down at Alex.

"One more slip up out of you, you're outtahere. It's a shit economy, and a fucking monkey can do your job. You understand?"

After they punched the clock, they walked out into the parking lot. It was early evening, and from the surrounding industrial environment, Alex could easily tell that he was in Cleveland. He had grown up here, and the factories surrounding the one he came out of, with their flaming smoke stacks and piles of industrial metals and salts, were easy enough to identify.

In the enormous parking lot, Teddy nodded to a nearby blue car that was idling.

"Yo Mr D," he shouted and raised up his hand.

The man in the car rolled his window down and said, "Hey Teddy, you staying out of trouble?" Alex saw that the man was his father, Ron, who had blonde hair and wore a full white beard.

"Of course I am. Not sure about this guy here, though," he said, motioning to Alex.

"Hey son," he said, laughing politely at Teddy's joke.

"Hello Dad," Alex said, wondering why his father was picking him up. Was something wrong with his car? What happened to California? To the island? To writing?

"I'll catch you guys later," Teddy said as he headed towards the bus stop.

"Yeah, have a nice night man," Alex said, and entered his dad's vehicle.

L

During the drive, Alex had so many questions that he had a hard time picking which ones to ask. Could he even trust this guy sitting next to him? It looked like his dad, and sounded like his dad. The guy even gripped the steering wheel in his usual white-knuckled, ten-and-two kind of way.

"How was work?" Ron asked him.

"Fine, I guess." Alex responded, not really sure what to make of his time at the factory. Ron nodded in understanding as they got stopped at the railroad tracks by the mechanical arm coming down at the crossing.

They sat there in silence for a moment.

Alex quickly became lost in the rhythmic chugga-a-lug of the freight train speeding by them. The locomotive blew its whistle as it passed, a sound he knew well, but as if from a distant dream.

His mother's ashes had been scattered further along these very railroad tracks, down where its metal rails met up with the bend in the Cuyahoga River that rested in the valley behind his childhood home. He had avoided these tracks ever since the day of her funeral. But here he was, being forced by the mechanical hand of the railroad crossing to come to terms with them.

"I saw Mom."

Alex said, not meaning to bring the subject up exactly like that. It was almost as if his subconscious pushed it out of his mouth without consulting any other part of his brain. His father turned to look at him.

"What do you mean you saw your mom? Like in a dream?"

"Not exactly. More like—"

"—A ghost?"

"No, more like a place in between time and timelessness."

"I'm not sure that I follow you, son," Ron said, bewildered. And at this point, Alex decided that he might as well confide in this man. What other choice did he have but to try and tell him everything?

"What I'm about to tell you, Dad, I don't exactly understand myself. I will try and explain it as best I can, though. You should maybe let me finish before you jump in, if that's okay."

"Okay Alex, sure," he said as the gate lifted and they drove on towards home.

And then he told his father everything. About Stella, the tunnel and the room, outer space, the Chaos, California, Candace, and the island. By the time he was done recounting everything to his father, they had made it back home and had been sitting in the garage for over an hour.

Ron did not interrupt his son even once. And when Alex had finished talking, he took a moment to process it.

"Did your mother say anything about me?"

Alex did not expect that response, but was touched by it nonetheless. If anything, it was all the confirmation he needed that this man was actually his father.

"I've been through so much, I honestly can't remember. I seem to recall her saying something about missing all of us, but she was different. Not cold, but not exactly human, either."

"Do you realize that you're talking like you're from some other version of reality?"

"That's kind of what I'm trying to say, Dad. I think I am. And in the reality that I know, I do not work in a factory. I am still a student and I live with Stella. But everything else is the same, at least I think."

"But Alex, even if what you are saying is somehow true, which I have a hard time believing since you've been living with me and working at the factory for years now, I've never even once heard you mention a girl named Stella, let alone live with anyone by that name."

"But that's impossible," his head was spinning. "Did I even go to university down in Columbus?"

"Well, yeah."

"Why do I work at the factory then?"

"It's a terrible economy. You're lucky to have any job at all with an English degree. I know MBA's out of work."

"Can you take me to Columbus then? She's gotta be down there still. She has to be."

"Sure, but it's gotta wait till this weekend. I'm swamped over at the bank and—"

"—Well what day is it today?"

"Tuesday."

"I'll just drive then. Where is my car anyways?"

"You haven't had a car since your license got suspended, but I'm sure you don't remember that in your new version of reality either."

"Suspended? For what?"

"Driving drunk. For the *fifth* time, but maybe that's why you don't recall."

"What? I'd *never* do that. C'mon dad, you know that."

"I didn't think you would either, but then after the third time—"

"Something's definitely not right here," Alex insisted.

"Or ask your brother. He's dropping off some laundry in about an hour."

My brother. Of course. He'll be able to help me clear this up, Alex thought.

LI

While he waited for his brother Eric to arrive, Alex decided to search around the house for clues. Anything that would just pop out at him as different from what he remembered. Not necessarily the color of the paint on the walls or carpeting of any individual room, or even for that matter, rearrangement or additions to furniture. Those kinds of things could change within any given house at any given moment. People decided to move things around all the time in hopes that it would make them feel better, or even just on a whim. Alex was thinking more along the lines of a permanent change. Like for instance, did he suddenly have an additional sibling in this present reality that he would find situated beside Eric and himself in an old family portrait? His father Ron matched his recollection of him, but would his brother when he got there? Was his mother the same woman who he had met with in the Chaos, and still had present in his memories? Were her ashes scattered in the same exact spot of the Cuyahoga River? Alex knew where the spot was supposed to be, about two miles back into the valley that started right behind his home. He could easily walk there. The real question was if he went back there by himself, would he be able to tell if she had been laid to rest there? Would some feeling magically come over him while he was there to reassure him? Did the spot itself even exist in this history?

But he was scared for some reason. Scared that going there would confirm a nagging fear of his that she no longer existed in any reality, that Chaos had made good on his threat despite the fact that Alex went through the portal. Maybe it was a trick? Maybe if he would have tried harder at fighting Chaos? Though he whipped him around like a rag doll, the King could not seem to kill Alex. Maybe he could have played up on that vulnerability.

What would he even have been able to do with his mother if he had saved her from Chaos' clutches? Certain laws of nature surely would have prevented him from dragging her out of the Chaos and back into eternity, or for that matter, taking her back into the present with him…right? But then again, he should have at least tried. She did tell him to go through the portal, though. He had only jumped in at her insistence. And didn't the fact that he still had memories of her prove that she still existed on some plane somewhere? The same goes for Stella, of course, but she had not even died. Stella was totally alive somewhere within time. Regardless of what his father said. Maybe her seeming disappearance could be blamed on the portal, too. If so, how could he go back through it or reverse it?

In the bottom drawer of the hutch in the living room, Alex found a pile of old family portraits and pictures from big events like vacations and first days of school. Each photo confirmed the memory of the family he had always known himself to be a part of. His mom, his dad, his brother and him – with no additions or subtractions. And he recognized the location of most of the pictures. The album from their trip to Myrtle Beach, the site of his first communion, etc.

The photograph that held his interest at the moment was one of his family standing next to a canon at an eighteenth century naval fortification on the coast of the Caribbean Sea at Puerto Rico. It looked out over steep cliffs that must have been very daunting to whatever enemy dare lay siege to it way back when.

"Remember how in that guy's taxi, even though it was a hundred degrees, he wouldn't open the windows?" his brother Eric asked from behind him.

"I thought I was going to puke all over you."

"So did I, man."

Eric had very blonde hair and was slightly taller than his older brother. He was holding a bag of dirty laundry that he placed down by the couch. He surveyed his brother for a moment, then said,

"Did you really see Mom?"

This did not feel like a trap. There was no judgment in Eric's voice. Only earnestness.

"Yes. I did."

"Where exactly?"

Alex had to assume that their father told Eric something about the Chaos over the phone before he got here.

"It was in this in-between place. It was very dark. But when I saw her, she had such a lovely light around her."

"Like an angel?"

"Yeah, kind of like that. No halo or anything, though."

Eric was grappling with his feelings on faith and loss and love through the prism of a young man who was a young boy back when his mother had passed away.

"What did she say to you?"

"That there is a certain numbness to death. But she, on some level at least, misses all of us. As much as a spirit is capable of such things."

"It really gives me some comfort, the idea of you being able to see her again. Makes me think that maybe I'll get to talk to her again. And Dad might not admit it to you, but I know he feels the same way about it."

Alex was caught off-guard by his brother's acceptance, and did not mean to be insensitive, but also at the same time had to know,

"Did Dad mention Stella to you?"

Eric silently nodded his head in the affirmative.

"And?"

"And I'm not sure that I know who she is exactly. Sorry."

"I don't understand it, but I'm not surprised."

"Look man, just because I don't know her doesn't mean she doesn't exist or something. You don't know every girl I've ever been with."

"Yeah, I suppose not."

"Dad told me you think she's in Columbus, right?"

"That's where I last saw her, before my little journey."

"Then I'll take you there, and we'll find her. We'll leave tomorrow morning."

"Great, thanks man."

"I'll swing by here, say, at 8?"

"Sounds good."

LII

It had now been hours since Eric was supposed to pick Alex up. Alex tried calling his brother several times, but could only reach his voicemail. Despite message after increasingly impatient message, his phone calls were not returned.

So what were his options then? His brother might still show up, or at least call him back. His father would be able to take him in a couple of days. But that was too long to wait. And Teddy, he just took the bus. Maybe some old high school buddy or something.

He went online down in the den and started searching for names of old friends, but produced no results. Nor did he get any hits when he searched for either Stella or himself. When he tried his brother and his father, two people he knew he had just seen, and did not come up with anything either, he started feeling like maybe he was trapped in some bizarre half-way world. Not real, not fake, just somewhere in between, or not fully formed or something. If he went down to Columbus, would there even be a city there for him to search? The city appeared to have an online presence, and from the looks of it, was the same place he remembered from when he lived there.

If he had any money, he had no idea how to retrieve it. Even if he did, it didn't much matter. There were no plane tickets available from Cleveland to Columbus within the next month, and the only bus that ran between the two cities already left this morning, and would not run again for a week. Might as well wait for dad at that point. Alex briefly considered hitchhiking, but knew that Stella would be against that in any reality. About the only other mode he could think of was train. The old freighter that ran through the valley behind his house only carried cargo, though. There was a very small-scale passenger rail system in Cleveland, but he did not live near any of its depots. And the furthest south that train went was to Akron.

The thought occurred to him that Stella might be with some alternate version of himself, or somebody else entirely. Either way, he would have no choice but to kill whoever it was if he encountered them with her. He wasn't sure exactly what his next move would be, but came to the quick realization that for the time being, he was stuck.

LIII

Not having anything else to do, Alex continued his investigation into trying to find something from the past that would shed light onto his present situation. About the best he could do were some old baseball mitts, graded tests and papers from elementary school, and loads more of the family pictures. Strangely, he recognized in every single picture a place that he had definitely been at some point in his life. But no signs of Stella, even in these.

His phone rang. It was Eric.

"Where are you?" Alex answered the phone.

"It's the craziest story, Alex. I'm actually in Milwaukee—" his brother started.

"—Milwaukee? What about Columbus?"

"I know, its just that, on the way home from dad's yesterday, I met this chick outside my apartment and—"

"—Are you coming back?"

"Yeah, eventually, but I think we're in love."

"Um, well, that's cool and all, but—"

"—Look bro, I gotta go. I'll take you in a couple of days, though, I promise."

Though disappointed, Alex could hardly begrudge him for acting spontaneously for love's sake. "Okay, talk to you later man," he said and they both hung up.

He was holding a picture of his mother and him, circa junior high. It was a marching band picture, and he was posing with his trombone before the first home game. A big fat mosquito landed on the photo and covered both of their faces up. He stared at the mosquito for a few moments, and remembered the one who bit him before he started his journey.

LIV

Standing in the meat aisle at the supermarket that was just down the street, Alex surveyed the cuts of lamb. Without paying too much attention to the quality of the meat, he threw a flank into his shopping cart. Next, he picked up a slab of ribs, ground beef, a few chicken breasts, sausage links, eggs, and some sugar. That was about all he'd be able to carry home for now. The cashier said something about it being a nice day, to which Alex politely agreed. He paid for it using the forty dollars that his father had placed on the kitchen table before he left for work, with instructions for Alex to buy himself some groceries.

He ran the plastic bags of food up to his bedroom, and placed them on the floor by his bed. He went across the hallway to the bathroom and brought the hamper into his closet. Calmly, he threw all of his clothing into the hamper, and then placed all the hangars under his bed. All that was left in the closet was an old oak cabinet. He placed the bags of food onto the top of the cabinet.

Removing the plastic wrapping from the flank of lamb proved messy, and blood and fat dripped all over the closet and the cabinet. Next, he clumped the ground beef up into balls and threw it at the walls. He did the same with the eggs, yoke yellow oozing into every nook and cranny. The cold pink chicken breasts were placed into the cabinet's drawers, covered in sugar. The ribs were placed on the floor, and the sausage links hung from the empty clothes rail. Then he opened the closet window slightly more than a crack, and poured the rest of the

213

sugar over everything. When he closed the closet door, he made sure it was good and tight, and stoppered the base of the door with a few towels.

LV

After a few hours, he removed the towels and opened the door. Even before he opened it, the stench was unbearable. A pandemonium of insects was flying around the bloody, decaying meat. He could barely breathe in there without gagging. Gasping for fresh air, he opened the window wider and knelt down below it. He took off his clothing and offered his skin for a free suck. Some of them sunk their jagged jaws into his flesh. At first, when only a dozen or so mosquitoes flocked to his body, he could feel each individual bite as it happened. In a few minutes he was covered with them, though, and all of their bites blended into one overall numbness.

After letting them feed for around an hour or so, and having not been transported back into outer space or to Stella or to the chaos or anything, he wiped all the bugs off his skin and exited the closet, quite swollen.

LVI

As he lay there on the family room couch, since he did not feel it would be possible to fall asleep in his wretchedly putrid room, he realized that he was actually supposed to work the next day. Looks like he'd be calling in sick, because he had no intention of ever going back to that place again. His father might try to make him go, though, as Ron was always a huge proponent of the benefits of an honest day's work. And it was only a matter of time before he realized that his son built a mosquito cave in the closet. He'd have to clean that up sooner than later.

Despite Alex's attempts at sleeping, he could not keep his mind from racing. Candace kept creeping back into his mind. He had not even sort of done right by her. She was a good person, and had a lot of love to give. How could he have taken her for granted? What if she was his real love, and Stella was only a figment of his imagination? If only his mother was still alive, he would ask her for advice. She always knew how to calm him down and give him hope when there appeared to be none. So he resolved to take a trip down to the spot where they scattered her ashes. He had avoided the spot for long enough. And the fresh air might do him some good.

***

By the time he got down into the valley, his head already felt clearer. He had concluded during his walk, that his only real choice was to be patient. He would wait for his father to take him down to Columbus in a few days, and in the meantime, maybe he'd actually go work at the factory. It might provide him with a diversion, while not wholly pleasant; at least it would occupy his mind where only confusion currently existed.

As he got to the point where the river meets up with the tracks, things started to look familiar. He could see the bend that had been etched into his memory so long ago.

When he got to the scattering spot, he recognized it immediately. He had no doubts whatsoever that the spirit of his mother was still present, despite Chaos' efforts. Watching the water as it seemed to flow in every direction at once, a gentle breeze passed through the trees, and he was content in interpreting it as a message from his mom that everything would be okay.

In the distance, he heard the whistle of the oncoming freighter. Within moments it was roaring alongside of him, all tagged up with bright graffiti. He walked alongside the tracks and couldn't help but to count the railroad cars as they passed by him. It was a long train, and each car seemed to be carrying the same cargo – some sort of raw material. And then he remembered learning back in grade school that it was iron ore, and that it was sent south for smelting or something or another, before it ultimately headed west. And as the train whistled again, he realized that it specifically went to Grove City, a suburb of Columbus. Oh my god, that was it. This was his ride down there. How could he have forgotten this train went to Columbus?

Only ten cars or so were left before it would pass him by completely. There was no time to think about it, he had to act. He got a running start, said a silent prayer of thanks to his mother, and leapt onto the speeding train. His hands grabbed onto the cold metal bar that ran alongside the back of the caboose. He had not meant to go for the caboose, but to the cart right before it, which happened to be open. Having misjudged the velocity of the train, though, he was just able to grab a hold of the caboose.

Alex held onto the rail just barely with his left hand, and found that the train was still moving fast enough that the force of it prevented him from grabbing on with the other hand. His footing wasn't very good, either. The ledge he was standing on couldn't be more than a foot or two wide, and since his right shoe was muddy from the woods, it kept slipping off.

The wind felt wet against his skin, and now moved with more force. And then seemingly out of nowhere, the lightning struck! And the thunder roared! The clouds opened up, and the rain poured down on him. The water made it hard to grip the pole he was holding, and the ledge became all but impossible to stand on.

Sensing the ever-growing futility of the ledge, Alex pushed off of it with his left foot so that it sprung the rest of him towards the pole. He clasped it with his free hand, and held on for dear life.

The rain beat down on him and tried to get between his hands and the pole, but he did not waver. He could have kept holding on until the train stopped, or at least slowed down, had it not been for the upcoming tunnel that ran through the valley's rocky ledges. Realizing that his body would slice in half when the train passed through, Alex let go before the tunnel's mouth.

He rolled down the muddy slope below, and kept rolling as it ended at the bank of the river. There was no rock or tree or anything like that to stop him, though, so his momentum took him right into the river itself.

The current carried Alex downstream. It was swift, and Alex could not fight it. He tried to resist it for a few minutes, but in those minutes, all of his energy was sapped out of him. The coldness and the power were just too much for him to withstand. He succumbed to the river's sway and simply gave in.

He was headed for a waterfall, when a red flame rose up from the Cuyahoga and consumed him.

***

Alex found himself in a small, empty room with green walls. The one wall was very bright. He went towards it, and saw that it was actually a window.

He looked though it, and saw Stella standing before the red-orange, cartoon man that was graffiti'd onto the wall of the tunnel beneath the university art building. She placed her hand on his right spiral eye. She seemed to be studying it.

Alex tried his best to get her attention by kicking and screaming at the thick window separating them. She did not appear to see or hear him. The red spiral eye started glowing, and then spinning in a circle off of the wall. It snaked around Stella like smoke, and grabbed a hold of her leg.

It pulled her in towards the wall, and brought her through it. Once she was through, the eye stopped glowing, and Alex was left looking out into the empty tunnel. He realized then, that he had finally made it into the room.

THE END.

ACKNOWLEDGMENTS

I would like to thank all of my friends and family for all of their love and support, especially my smart, beautiful, and patient wife Leslie. I miss you Mom.

Cover Design: Nick Dyko
Editor: Leslie Dyko

ABOUT THE AUTHOR

Brian Dyko is a writer who lives in Los Angeles, CA. He is originally from Cleveland, OH, and encourages you to go there to check out Lake Erie. He graduated from The Ohio State University in 2007 in English Literature, and received his MFA in Writing for The Screen and Television from The University of Southern California's School of Cinematic Arts in 2010.

Despite his best efforts to exist in several dimensions at once, he is currently located on the earth.

TUNNEL is Brian's first novel, and is the first part of a three-book series. In the meantime, you can keep up with him on Twitter @prettyponytime

Or check out the official TUNNEL Facebook page for more stories and info!